"This is one night I'm not likely to forget."

"Stop a minute and catch your breath," Simon said.

"You all right?" he asked, close enough that his breath warmed her already overheated face.

"Uh, huh," she lied.

He ran the back of his knuckles along her cheek, making her catch her breath. "You're trembling."

"I'm not used to the exercise."

"Liar."

He was crowding her against the tree she leaned against, still touching her with one hand, while his other was flattened on the tree trunk behind her. Though his body was inches from hers, she imagined them clinging together...naked.

Vaguely remembering the reason they'd been forced to run into the swamp, she whispered, "Don't you have anything more productive to do?"

"Well, then..."

His head dipped slow enough that it gave her time to duck if that was what she wanted to do.

She didn't....

Dear Reader,

As a writer, I love nothing more than throwing my heroes and heroines to the precipice of danger, to make ordinary people fight the worst villains and win. For me, it's a celebration of the human spirit, the discovery of untapped strengths that I am certain we all possess if only we can find the courage to reach deep inside ourselves.

A Lover Awaits is book three of my Seven Sins series. For this series, I've chosen to raise the stakes, to push my heroes and heroines to the emotional edge at the same time they are fighting for their very existence. In the midst of mortal danger, they must wrestle with equally destructive inner demons and take back their lives…and in doing so, be rewarded with a love for all time.

Let me know how you enjoy their stories at P.O. Box 578279, Chicago, IL 60657-8297.

Patricia Rosemoor

A Lover Awaits
Patricia Rosemoor

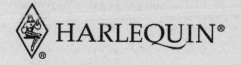

TORONTO • NEW YORK • LONDON
AMSTERDAM • PARIS • SYDNEY • HAMBURG
STOCKHOLM • ATHENS • TOKYO • MILAN • MADRID
PRAGUE • WARSAW • BUDAPEST • AUCKLAND

Thanks to Elaine Sima for her spectacular house which
now belongs to me via Phoebe <g>;
to Elaine and Sherrill Bodine for introducing me to a
fascinating new setting; and to Dennis Perry for helping
me work out some of the crime details.

ISBN 0-373-22499-0

A LOVER AWAITS

Copyright © 1999 by Patricia Pinianski

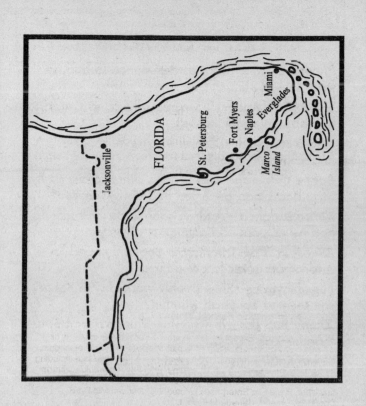

FLORIDA

Jacksonville

St. Petersburg

Fort Myers

Naples

Marco
Island

Everglades

Miami

CAST OF CHARACTERS

Phoebe Grant—She was determined to find her sister's murderer.

Simon Calderon—He was equally determined…to find absolution for himself.

Audra Laughlin—Did her insatiable appetites finally take their toll?

Boone Calderon—Did Simon's twin brother really have bad blood as Simon had always feared?

Vance Laughlin—Audra's soon to be ex-husband had never stopped fighting the divorce.

Blair Ratcliffe—The fiancée Boone dumped for Audra had never forgiven him.

Elise Navarro—She not only worked with Boone, she seemed obsessed with him.

Jimmy Bob Dortch—The handyman knew more than he was saying.

Kevin Saltis—Phoebe's partner had an even deeper insight to Phoebe's sister than she did.

Prologue

"Our newest subject is Phoebe Grant," Zoe Declue announced, fingering the folder she'd set on the table between them, then suddenly withdrawing her hand.

Alex Gotham stared at his collaborator, fascinated by the haze of pink creeping up her neck and beneath the blunt cut of her silvery chin-length hair.

"What's the rush?" he asked. "We haven't even ordered yet."

Zoe started, her gaze darting around the room until it lit on a nearby waitress, arms loaded with a tray of food. Her deep green eyes flashed open wide, almost as if she'd just remembered she'd asked him to meet her at a restaurant rather than at her office, Alex thought.

"I, uh, know what I want, and it might be a while," she murmured in that soft voice that enveloped him in its silky cocoon. "I thought we could get a head start on the, uh…topic for Chapter Three."

Lust.

How odd that she avoided saying it, Alex thought. As odd as her insisting they meet in a public place…as odd as her wearing a steel-gray suit designed for a more mature, harder personality. He'd never seen her in anything but softly neutral outfits touched with some warm hue that made him suspect an intriguing sensuality hidden beneath her cool exterior.

Hidden…

Alex couldn't help himself. He said, "Why don't you give me your take on the topic before getting into specifics," just to see her reaction.

"Yes, well…lust…gratification without involvement. A sin that denies feelings deeper than the physical."

The becoming color spread to her cheeks, making Alex suspect that Zoe was embarrassed.

Perhaps a bit prudish?

They'd been working together only a short time and he didn't know her well enough to say…

A research psychologist, Zoe Declue had approached him to write a book about the Seven Deadly Sins—a humanistic examination of pride, envy, wrath, sloth, avarice, gluttony and lust. She wanted to demonstrate how these sins kept a person isolated from society and therefore from loving freely. And through the cooperation of her colleagues across the country—and given the written permission of their patients who would remain anonymous—they were able to focus on true-life narratives. Each chapter would tell the story of a single person who'd found a second chance at life after recognizing and rising above one of the emotion-based sins.

Writing the book with her was *his* second chance,

and for that, Alex was grateful. Several years before as a moderately successful investigative reporter, he'd been thrown into stardom with the publication of *Lost Youth,* his highly touted nonfiction look into the world of runaway teens. Unfortunately, his life had taken an unexpectedly gruesome turn, and it had been downhill from there…straight into the depths of a liquor bottle.

But he was coming back.

Work was keeping him sober, one day at a time.

Alex wondered about Zoe's sin against herself. More than once, he'd suspected her interest in the project was as personal as it was professional.

What would *she* have to resolve so that she could find fulfillment and happiness?

Thinking that it was only a matter of time before he found out, Alex let her off the hook and returned to the subject of their next chapter.

"So this Phoebe Grant…she was promiscuous?"

"That's not exactly what I meant to imply." Zoe opened the folder. "Her story is far more complex."

"Aren't they all?" Alex murmured.

"Very early on, Phoebe became convinced that love was…well, the source of unhappiness for the women in her family."

Confused, he asked, "So she *rejected* men?"

"No, not at all. She merely decided that, um…" Zoe licked her lips. "…lust was preferable to love."

Again, he was struck by her surprising difficulty in broaching the topic. Wanting to explore that, he held himself in check instead. "So she chose to get her physical gratification without emotion."

"Exactly. Through therapy, Phoebe came to realize

that she'd actually been cheating herself of real happiness.''

''Sex therapy,'' Alex couldn't resist saying, just to see the soft color returning once again to Zoe's cheeks.

''Grief counseling,'' she countered. ''I told you it was complicated. Let me start from the beginning.''

He took the newspaper clipping she held out to him. The lurid headline read: Passion Ends in Murder-Suicide.

Chapter One

"Just in..." The anchorwoman's dark eyebrows arched beneath straight blond bangs. "Last Monday morning, the bodies of Boone Calderon and Audra Laughlin were found in his Marco Island home," she said.

A photo of the couple filled the television screen.

"While the investigation continues, authorities surmise the deaths to be a murder-suicide. The preliminary investigation indicates that Calderon shot his lover to prevent her from reconciling with her husband—successful Fort Myers businessman Vance Laughlin—before turning the gun on himself..."

The words from the newscaster's earlier broadcast echoed in Phoebe Grant's head until she wanted to scream, "Not true!"

A gust of wind howled through the palm fronds and threw fine wisps of hair in her eyes as she picked her way through the aftermath of the tropical summer storm. Her dock shoes were soaked, her bare ankles and shins nicked by vegetation and other debris that littered the ground. Phoebe hardly noticed. Too aware of the pressure in her chest, of the rush of blood through her ears, of the knot in her stomach, she stopped and stared at the silhouette of the house.

For a moment, the dread filling her at the thought of entering made her waver in her purpose.

Even in the middle of the night, lights temporarily doused by electrical failure, moon swamped by diminishing storm clouds, she could see the structure clearly in her mind's eye: two stories high…pillars flanking the front doors…exterior the color of lust…

Sucking in the fetid air mixed with the strong odor of fish always left behind after a storm raged through the area, she forced her legs forward.

A warning hiss and a skittering sound—a big and heavy body quickly scrambling along the ground— followed by a loud *plunk* into the channel made her insides clutch. *Alligator.* The dangerous reptiles didn't usually hang out around here. This one had probably taken shelter from the storm. But where one gator lurked…

Not savoring the thought of an accidental meeting in the dark, Phoebe snapped on the flashlight she'd removed from her glove compartment and swept its beam over the area. A six-foot saw palmetto had been upended from its roots, a low hedge of lantana flattened, its crushed leaves releasing a spicy pungent aroma.

Nothing more threatening than debris.

Fishing her sister's extra set of house keys from her pocket, Phoebe hurried to the front door, released the lock and let herself inside.

What she expected to find, she couldn't say.

But something—anything—to prove the authorities wrong.

Boone hadn't killed Audra. Hadn't turned the gun on himself. She knew this deep in her heart. Her sister had been too happy. Had put too much stock in this relationship. No matter what Vance had told the authorities—no matter that he had played the contrite and grieving husband to the hilt—Phoebe knew Audra hadn't had any intention of reconciling.

So why the lie?

Vance was the one who had a reason to be jealous. Not that he'd ever needed a reason before, she grimly remembered. The man had been downright delusional.

And why wouldn't Detective Sandstrom believe her? He'd listened politely, had even promised to check it out, but she had the feeling he'd categorized her as being something less than a credible source. Too emotional.

She didn't want to think the other…that money could buy anything…anyone…even the men sworn to uphold justice.

Her brother-in-law had plenty of cash to spare. Had he bought off someone associated with the investigation? If she found evidence that might incriminate him, then what?

Phoebe only hoped she could trust Detective Sandstrom to do the right thing.

So she was inside. Now what?

She'd acted on instinct, not from plan. The late-night news broadcast had jolted her out of her shock-induced complacency. She hadn't taken the time to think things through.

What to look for?

A diary...

Audra had kept one from girlhood on, had ritualized recording her thoughts and emotions. Phoebe wished she'd remembered this when talking to the authorities, but even now, she was finding it difficult to remain clearheaded. Audra had been the only family she'd ever felt close to. Even now, tears threatened.

She pulled herself together and concentrated on her mission.

On leaving her husband, Audra had moved into their mother and stepfather's vacated winter townhouse in Naples. But after meeting Boone, she'd begun dividing her time between their place and his.

What was to say she hadn't brought the journal with her that fateful night?

It *could* be here, Phoebe reasoned.

Armed only with the flashlight, she moved away from the door. Luckily she'd been in the house several times before—often enough to know her way around. Its center was an atrium, the double-story rise split only by a suspended walkway, which connected the second-floor master suite on one side of the building with the guest rooms on the other.

She would start with Boone's bedroom.

Heading for the stairs, she paused at a hint of nearby movement. A mere whisper in the dark. She flashed the beam around the open living area and beyond, through the glass wall to the lanai. Nothing.

Maybe the sound had come from the private dock where the boat Boone had used to get to work every morning was anchored.

Another gator, she concluded.

Shaking off her unease, she climbed the steps to the master suite. The sitting room, bedroom and bath bore witness to the investigation. Torn up. And yet the sign of a lovers' tryst was still evident. Perfumed silk sheets. Candles burned to nubs. Flowers everywhere. Shriveled. Dead.

Just like her sister and the man she'd loved.

Though they hadn't died here.

Audra had been found floating facedown in the swimming pool, while Boone had clung to the edge, his right hand and leg dangling in the water. The gun had sunk to the bottom of the pool.

A lump caught in her throat even as she heard yet another sound, nearly certain this one came from somewhere within the house.

What if she wasn't alone?

What if the real murderer had returned to the scene of the crime?

Phoebe nearly choked on her own stupidity. She should have waited for daybreak. She shouldn't have come alone.

Deciding to get out while the getting was good, to come back the next morning with Kevin—she'd twist her partner's arm if necessary—she snapped off the flashlight and sidled out of the bedroom. Ears attuned to the night, she cautiously started back down the stairs, careful to make no sound herself.

Not that she could hear much above the thunder of her blood rushing through her ears.

Dry-mouthed, she barely breathed until she reached the bottom of the steps. She flew across the still-dark room toward the front door, a ragged, relieved breath rattling her chest as she reached for the knob.

Her hand hit something solid...something whip-cord hard...*something distinctly not wood.*

With a smothered cry, she tried fleeing in the opposite direction—toward the lanai—but before she knew what was happening, a hard grip on her shoulder spun her around and shoved her to the floor. A heavy weight descending on her pinned her neatly in place.

"Get off me!" she cried, flashlight and nails flying toward his face.

As if by instinct rather than sight—unless he had a cat's ability to see in the dark—he caught both her wrists and plunged her arms up over her head, somehow managing to remove the flashlight from her hand in the process.

He...definitely a man...the murderer returned to the scene of the crime?

And there she lay...her soft belly exposed... vulnerable.

Phoebe tried bucking him, kneeing him, kicking him. All she got for her trouble was frustration. And then he easily grasped both her wrists in one hand and flashed her own light in her face.

"Who the hell are you?" he demanded. "And what is it you want here?"

Her lungs deflated by his weight, she could hardly squeak, "Me?"

"You," he repeated even as the power came back on and the room lit up like a Christmas display.

Her eyes squinched automatically against the unexpected, nearly blinding light, but she forced them open wide and focused on her attacker.

Loose strands of dark brown hair tumbled over a high, narrow forehead...heavy-lidded, almost black eyes (bedroom eyes, Audra had called them)... straight, prominent nose...hollow, beard-shadowed cheeks...teeth bared threateningly above a square jaw...definitely alarming...and yet as handsome as sin...

Her mouth dropped open. "Boone..." rasped between her suddenly stiff lips. She blinked, but the apparition didn't change.

The man who'd been declared dead along with her sister continued to glare down at her.

Ghost was the first thought that came to mind.

Hoax the second, for this was no spirit but a flesh-and-blood man.

But she'd seen Boone Calderon buried!

A closer audit of his features revealed subtle differences—imperfections—the most notable of which was a scar threading his stubbled chin. Understanding hit her with a jolt. She'd known Boone had a brother who rarely came out of his swamp, though no one had ever mentioned he was a twin.

"You're Simon Calderon!"

Her preconception of him made the statement an

accusation. Heir to his brother's estate, he hadn't even shown for the funeral.

"I know who *I* am—"

"Get off!"

"—which gives you one up on me."

"At least I'm not crushing the life out of you," she gasped out, then, because she figured she had to if she ever wanted to breathe normally again, added, "I'm Phoebe Grant. Audra's sister."

With obvious reluctance, he released her hands, his calloused thumbs lightly flicking against her sensitive inner wrists as he drew back. An unfamiliar and unwelcome sensation swamped her. Phoebe trembled and fought the instinct to punch him for giving her such a scare. Even now, sitting back on his haunches, Simon Calderon made her uneasy. His jeans-clad thighs hugged her hips like a lover's…though his passionless features were anything but loving. Finally, to her relief, he rose, allowing her to scramble to her feet.

"You didn't answer my question."

Glaring up at him, she said, "I identified myself."

"About why you're here."

"I was looking for something."

"What?"

Not knowing why she didn't tell him about the diary, she said, "Anything…a lead to the murders…"

Arms crossed over his chest, silent, he waited.

"You must have heard the official theory," Phoebe said. "The authorities got it wrong."

If she expected Simon to join in, to curse the stupid fools, she was disappointed. It was almost as if…

Forehead wrinkling, she said, "A killer is running around loose."

"More likely dead of a self inflicted gunshot."

She gaped. "You can't possibly believe that."

"Why not?"

"Boone was your brother! Your twin. Surely you knew him better than anyone."

"Exactly." His simple statement chilled her.

Phoebe stared, wondering how she could have mistaken him for Boone. Her sister's lover had never been so judgmental. Had never looked so closed off from human emotion. Simon hadn't even come to the funeral. He didn't seem to be grieving for his brother now. He appeared as cold-blooded as the alligators with whom he lived cheek by jowl in his swamp.

"You really think Boone was capable of murder?"

He turned away. "I *know* what my brother was capable of."

She grabbed his arm to stop him from walking away. He glanced down at her hand, then slowly raised his gaze to her face, staring at her as if she were a pesky insect. But when she let go, he stayed put.

"I don't understand."

"You don't need to."

"Yes," she argued, thinking of her sister—of the good-hearted if misguided young woman whose life had been snuffed out by a bullet. "I do."

His renewed silence distressed her. As did his penetrating gaze. Phoebe stared back, willing him to say what was on his mind.

"Before you leave," Simon finally said, "I'll take

the keys." When she stared stupidly at him, at a loss for words, he added, "The ones you used to get inside." Those bedroom eyes traveled ever so slowly down her flesh—face to throat to breasts to stomach—finally settling on her right hip where the keys made a bulge in her shorts pocket. "I guess I can fetch them myself."

He reached out as if he meant to do exactly that.

Unnerved, already violated by his intense gaze and unwilling to take any more from him, Phoebe slapped his hand away, fetched the keys and shoved them into his chest. *Hard.* His lips twitched as he took them from her, his subtle amusement fueling her temper.

"Boone made Audra happy," she hotly informed him. "She loved your brother and for once I approved of her choice in men. He was one of the most decent guys I've ever met. He didn't try to control her. Didn't manipulate her. Didn't abuse her. Why would he kill her?"

A flicker behind those dark eyes told her she'd gotten to him, and yet he spoke without a hint of emotion. "Maybe it was like the authorities said and your sister meant to go back to her husband."

"She wouldn't have."

Even as she made the denial, Phoebe knew a moment's doubt. Like their mother before her, Audra had never been astute in her choice of men—not until Boone. And Vance—Audra's biggest mistake—had always been able to exert too much power over her. Unwilling to believe such nonsense, Phoebe shook away the disturbing qualm.

"More likely her husband did it," she said.

"Out of jealousy?"

"Something like that. Vance Laughlin never lets go of a possession until he's done with it. He wasn't done with my sister."

The very coldness of Simon's voice ate its way up her spine when he asked, "Laughlin physically abused her?"

If Vance had ever hit her sister, Audra had never admitted as much. But then, abused women rarely did. "I know she was afraid of him."

Vance Laughlin demanded perfection in everything. How many times had Audra fearfully recounted his displeasure if she bought the wrong wine or wore a dress he disliked?

"Not the same thing," Simon said.

"Abuse has many faces." Ugly faces that she'd recognized even as a child. "Vance relishes exercising his power at every opportunity...especially when he's been drinking."

Again something flicked deep within Simon's eyes. *Pain?*

So he wasn't completely invulnerable, Phoebe realized, quick to take advantage.

"What if Boone didn't do it?" she demanded. "Don't you want to clear his good name?"

"What other people think doesn't matter."

Other people...

"What about you?" she asked. "About what you think? Don't you want to know the truth?"

He didn't have to answer. His eyes did that for him.

"If I'm right," she pressed on, "what about the *real* murderer? Shouldn't he be stopped? Don't you want justice?'' At this last remark, Simon's dark expression made Phoebe fear she'd lost him.

''It's not up to us to mete out justice—''

''That's not what I said. Or meant. I'm talking about digging for the truth, and once we find it, handing it over to the authorities.''

To someone who would listen with an open mind. Someone who would believe her.

For a moment, Phoebe thought she had Simon's attention again. Just as quickly, the glimmer of humanity she'd glimpsed receded...leaving her with the cold, uncaring shell of a person she'd sized him up to be in the first place.

His next words confirmed it.

''Don't let the door hit you on your way out.''

Stubbornly, she held her ground. ''Look, if you don't want to get involved, don't. But I'm not giving up.'' Even figuring she was arguing with a wall, she said, ''As long as I'm here, why not let me—''

''You wasted the drive, Phoebe, so give up.''

She let out a frustrated sound and shook her head. ''I'll never give up. And I don't understand.''

This time he didn't argue, merely moved in on her so close she caught her breath. Barely enough room for a sheet of paper between them, she stared at his chin, at the small scar, because it should have been safer than meeting those bedroom eyes, when, in fact, she didn't feel safe at all.

She felt...what?...surely not attracted to him?

Rather, she acknowledged a recognition of Simon's intensity...of his inner strength...and especially of some dark force lurking below the surface that frightened her.

Just when she couldn't stand it a moment longer, he reached past her. The door clicked open. She met his gaze and was surprised to see amusement—like when he'd forced her to turn over the keys.

Tempted to stay put, Phoebe knew it was useless. He'd throw her out bodily if he had to. Still, she wouldn't turn tail and run, as instinct was urging her.

She backed off slowly, carefully, placing one foot behind the other until she'd passed through the doorway. There she stopped, gaze still connected with his, willing Simon to change his mind.

What he did instead was slam the door in her face.

SIMON'S AMUSEMENT faded the moment the door swung shut.

He waited for her to leave, but Phoebe Grant was nothing if not obstinate.

Imagining her angular face, stubborn chin slightly cocked, straight nose tilted, wide-spaced hazel eyes (the left punctuated by a mole at its outer corner) focused on him—judging him—he tensed. He answered to no one. Assuredly not to some strange woman who wanted to tell him how he should feel about his own brother's death.

What did she know about the dark recesses of the human soul?

Her sister had died, as well. Murdered. That qualified her for something, he guessed.

He sensed her waiting. For him to relent? To invite

her back inside, not only into the house, but into his life?

The hell he would!

One minute stretched to two, two to three, and still she made no move to leave. Simon clenched his jaw. Reaching out, he turned the dead bolt, hoping its snap was loud enough for her to hear on the other side.

Finally, he sensed her withdrawal, heard the whisper of her sneakers against the walkway. Finally, she gave up, albeit with reluctance, he was certain.

And he was left alone once more, exactly as he'd been inside for most of his life.

Boone's life was over...

His twin's probable suicide made Simon feel emptier than before.

Chapter Two

"So, you a native, or what?" Kevin Saltis asked the buxom blonde who perched on a bar stool across from him, while he made her a piña colada.

"A native of New Jersey." The young woman leaned in closer, offering him a view of her cleavage.

Kevin's dark eyes—his most tangible legacy from his Cuban grandfather—snapped with interest. "You're just visiting, then?"

"Working on my tan."

From her post at the nearby hostess's stand, Phoebe arched her eyebrows. *Burn* was more like it. The blonde's skin had the glow of raw meat. Too many tourists tended to barbecue themselves as if needing to prove they'd been to Florida—threat of skin cancer or no.

"Lookin' good," her fair-haired partner murmured, as Phoebe had heard him do dozens of times with dozens of uncomplicated women on dozens of hot, slow-moving days like this.

Kevin flexed his considerable muscle as he set the young woman's drink on the bar. Although he was only five foot ten, he was broad-shouldered and so brawny that he gave the impression of a much larger man. His infectious grin heightened his boy-next-door good looks. People took him for thirty, though in reality, Kevin Saltis would soon shake hands with the big four-o. That didn't stop him from going after young women. His striking out was a rare occurrence, and about the only thing guaranteed to darken his naturally sunny disposition.

Even now, he was murmuring, "Maybe you'd like someone to show you the nightlife…"

Irritated at being privy to the flirtation when she had a far more serious issue to discuss with him, Phoebe left the shelter of the overhang and drew closer to the dock.

Halfway out in the bay, a dolphin arched above the water, undoubtedly in pursuit of a fresh fish lunch. Preening on the end post of the pier, a pelican stretched its wings and sunned itself, odd-shaped beak lifted to the sky, whose clear blue sweep held no trace of yesterday's storm. Seagulls shrieked as they floated overhead, the scavengers already scouring the area for discarded people food.

Nearly midday.

The hot and humid breeze sweeping over her did little to dry the perspiration already dotting her body.

Florida in August could be murder…

Murder…Audra…

Hot tears sprang to the backs of her eyes and Phoebe concentrated on keeping them from falling. She wouldn't cry in public and humiliate herself, especially not here. What would her customers think?

The lunchtime crowd was drifting in. Work would occupy her mind. Drawing herself together, she found a smile from somewhere, seated a party of four beneath a ceiling fan, handed out menus and distributed glasses of ice water.

"Your waitress will be right with you," she promised, even as three cranky little kids accompanying an even crankier mother arrived.

Luckily, she was able to seat them inside, where the air-conditioning would cool off their tempers and the window view (hopefully) would keep the kids interested.

Tourists and locals alike frequented the Blue Crab Bar and Grill, known for its lunchtime special—softshell crab sandwiches. She and Kevin kept the menu simple, the food good and portions generous—and were rewarded by a steady, modestly lucrative business.

The place filled up fast. At some point, another lone young woman came in and greeted the one at the bar. She indicated they wanted a table. Before following Phoebe, the blonde gave Kevin a promising smile and a mouthed "later."

During a lull in the action, Phoebe drifted back to the bar, where her partner was filling a drink order. Picking up the conversation she'd tried to have with him prior to the blonde's entrance, she asked, "So what do you think I should do?"

"About what?"

"How soon we forget. Simon Calderon."

"You think he's good-looking?"

Frowning, she tried not to visualize the hollow-cheeked face that had haunted her sleep. "He looks exactly like Boone." Except for a few harder edges, and that scar. "I told you they were twins."

"But are you attracted to him?"

"What?"

"Is he your type?"

"Kevin-n-n..."

"Phe-e-ebs..."

Heat flaring up her neck, she glanced over her shoulder. Once assured no one was paying them any mind, she turned back to her partner.

"What's wrong with you? I'm trying to get some answers about my sister's murder and you're trying to set me up with a date."

"You could use more than a date." Setting drinks on a tray, Kevin wiggled his eyebrows at her. "You need some action, down and dirty. Get rid of some of that tension."

"My love life is none of your business."

Even as he demanded, *"What* love life?" she thought of dark bedroom eyes. For the moment regretting that she had so readily confided in a man who was her *business* partner, Phoebe muttered, "You're exasperating!"

"But cute, right?"

"Get serious."

"You want serious?" The boyish smile faded, to be replaced by an expression of concern. "Okay. As much as I know you're going to hate this...I think the cops got it nailed, Pheebs. For all his appearing to be a normal kinda guy, Boone Calderon coulda been a pint short. I think you're wasting your time."

He was right. She didn't like it. "Thanks a lot."

"But, I'm there for you," he added warmly. "Say the word and I'll help any way I can."

"Thanks," she said again, this time meaning it. "I'll let you know if I come up with something."

Kevin was her sounding board. Had been since the year before, when she'd inherited her father's half of the business. He'd quickly become her mentor. And her best buddy. Moving around so much while growing up had precluded a close relationship with anyone but her sisters—really only Audra—so making friends was difficult for her. Thankfully, Kevin hadn't let her social ineptness stand in his way. Also thankfully, she wasn't his type.

She'd choose a good friend over "a man" any day. She'd learned well by negative example.

SIMON LET MOST of the day drift by without accomplishing a thing. He'd meant to get in and out, do what he had to before disappearing back into his swamp, but life didn't always go as planned.

He found himself wandering the house, wondering. Trying to make sense of the senseless. Searching for a level playing field where there were only hills and curves.

Boone's home. Boone's possessions. Now all of it belonged to him.

Paul Hines had arrived at Calderon's Landing the day after the burial Simon had refused to attend (denial had long been his strong suit)…had informed him that he was Boone's sole beneficiary…had assured him that all would go smoothly through the courts.

As if he cared about *things*.

The lawyer had unsuccessfully hidden his amusement when Simon had said as much. He'd left a package of legal papers and several sets of keys and headed back to his office in Naples.

And Simon—compelled by a bond that few would understand—had reluctantly left his swamp.

His first stop had been the cemetery and his twin's graveside. No matter that he'd arrived in the midst of a tropical storm. He'd sat there all day, heedless of the wind and the rain and the mud...of anything but the past.

Reminiscing...reconnecting...remembering...

None of which would bring Boone back.

None of which gave Simon comfort.

Boone and Simon...Simon and Boone...identical... interchangeable...

Like faces...like bodies...like psyches?

If only the rain could have cleansed him, could have washed that question from his mind.

If only...

APPEARING UNANNOUNCED at Calderon Charters late that afternoon probably wasn't the smartest move Simon had ever made. Hell, it wasn't even one that he wanted to make. But the business was his now, at least until he decided what to do with it, and with ownership came obligation. The employees needed some sense of continuity, not to mention the assurance of a forthcoming paycheck.

The business was located directly on the docks at the mouth of Marco River, where the channel spilled into the Gulf of Mexico. The white stucco two-story structure with deep-blue-tiled roof sprawled about a hundred yards from the main pier where boats of every size and description from speedboats to luxury yachts were tied up.

The moment Simon opened the office door, all heads turned toward him, one by one, as if in slow motion. Eyes went wide. Voices stilled.

Making Simon wish he were anywhere but here.

"Madre de Dios!" came a choked female voice from the back of the room.

Simon zeroed in on the only woman present. Young and lovely, a thick dark plait hanging over one shoulder, she was elegant despite the simple orange sweater and white shorts that revealed long, slender limbs. Her features and coloring reflected a multicultural heritage he guessed to be Cuban-Anglo-African. Her soft brown eyes were awash with tears.

She stepped forward, her slender ringed hand outstretched in a beseeching manner. "Boone?"

Before Simon could correct her natural mistake, her thick lashes fluttered wildly and she crumpled to the floor.

"Elise!" The youngest of the men flew to her side, where he knelt and touched her face. His gelled crew-cut practically quivered with anger as, glaring at Simon, his tone accusing, he said, "She's out cold."

The extreme reaction prompted Simon to assume Elise was another of Boone's conquests.

"You're obviously the brother," an old salt said. Big and grizzled, he shoved his billed cap back along his receding hairline as if to give his rheumy blue eyes a clear field. "Two peas in a pod, eh?"

Exactly what Simon feared.

"Twins," he agreed.

A wizened black man in a striped T-shirt a couple of sizes too big raced to the cooler. "I'll get some water!"

Simon stood there, fighting his instinct to take charge of the situation. He was the interloper. The outsider. And he chose to maintain the status quo.

"Elise, it's all right." The young man was gently patting her cheek, his voice soft and reassuring. "You didn't see no ghost. It ain't Boone."

"C'mon, now, sweetheart, drink this," the skinny man said.

The men got the job done without him. Elise finally responded and opened her eyes. After she took the proffered sip of water, they got her to her feet.

"Sorry," she muttered, fingers clenching the cup of water as she faced Simon. "I-I'm so embarrassed."

"Don't be. I'm used to it."

"Having women faint on you?"

Thinking of Phoebe Grant, he said, "Having them mistake me for my brother."

Dark shadows beneath the young woman's eyes indicated lack of rest. And she couldn't control the tremor in her hand as she took another sip of water.

But a moment later, appearing steadier, she made the introductions.

Elise Navarro had been Boone's assistant, and ran the everyday workings of the office. The old salt, Magnus Hanson, was one of the charter captains, the scrawny man his mate Elijah Greer. And Corky Slotnik, a new hire straight out of the navy, was the one who'd come to her aid.

"I'm sure you'll want to see your office," she said, leading the way to the inner room.

"My *brother's* office."

Though her expression was questioning, he didn't explain.

While smaller than the outer room, Boone's office had the same feeling of spaciousness as his home. Desk and bookcases of pale wood flanked a light blue rug whose pattern was nautical. Two slim chairs were the mates to the executive job behind the desk, all upholstered with outlines of sailing ships. A long file cabinet placed against one wall was also of light wood, and had the feel of fine furniture. Its top surface was dotted with pieces of coral.

But the centerpiece of the office was the oversized window opposite the desk.

Simon stood before it a moment, connecting with the blue and green ribbons of water, the colors startling in their intensity so soon after a storm.

"Can I get you anything?" Elise asked.

"Not today. I just need a few minutes alone."

Staring out at the Gulf, allowing calm to wash over him, he knew his first moment of peace since the news of Boone's death had breached his world.

"You're going to sell, aren't you?"

Harmony shattered, Simon faced Elise, who'd stopped in the doorway. "I haven't decided yet. Maybe I'll let someone else run it."

She nodded and backed out.

Leaving Simon alone to contemplate the irony of his and Boone's lives.

They couldn't have been more different—or more identical.

While they'd rarely had contact as adults, they'd both lived on the water—he in the swamp, Boone on the ocean. They'd both made their living from tourists and local sportsmen—he with airboats, Boone with fishing boats.

Twins, living lives that were completely separate, and yet so similar.

How deep did that sameness go?

Fearing the dark side that he'd witnessed firsthand in his twin all those years ago, Simon was tempted to disappear back into his swamp where he could continue to avoid the past.

But the biggest part of his past had just died by his own hand, Simon thought.

Or had he?

Could Phoebe Grant know something she wasn't telling?

For his own sake, he wanted to believe that the authorities were wrong…that *he* was wrong…that his twin could have been a victim rather than a murderer…. Simon wondered what it would take to find out.

THE BLONDE RETURNED after the dinner-hour rush, just as Phoebe had expected.

One look at his newest conquest and Kevin suggested, "Why don't you call it a night? I can take care of things here and lock up."

Only two other couples were lingering over drinks. So why was she hanging around when she could...what?

A return trip to Boone Calderon's home was not an option. She no longer had the keys and if she tried breaking in, his brother might go to more drastic measures than just asking her to leave. He might have her arrested for trespassing.

Simon Calderon...closed off...unfeeling...

At least that's what he wanted her to think.

She couldn't forget the flicker of emotion he'd been quick to hide. He'd been hurting, not only from Boone's death, but from believing his twin capable of murder.

But why would he?

A question she was certain she'd never have answered.

Phoebe started, realizing that her partner and his love interest were making moon eyes at each other.

"You're sure you won't be too distracted to lock up?" she asked.

Kevin grinned. "Positive. I'm multitalented, you know. So go home. Go to bed. Sleep late. Don't even bother coming in tomorrow."

She quirked an eyebrow at him. "Trying to get rid of me?"

"Trying to take care of you."

"Uh-huh." While taking care of himself. Phoebe shook her head. "About tomorrow—" The thought of having yet another day to recover from the emotional trauma of her sister's death was tempting, and yet she feared not working would give her too much time to think. "—I'll let you know."

He waved her off. "Go."

Phoebe went...but not home.

Instead, when she jumped in her convertible, she decided to pass up home for Dolphin's Gate, the Naples closed community where Audra had been staying in their mother and stepfather's winter home.

The police had been there before her, of course. While not the crime scene, they nevertheless had searched the place, going through Audra's personal effects and papers, looking for some indication that all was not as it had seemed. They'd found exactly squat.

With failure almost a certainty, she still had nothing to lose. No way was she going to get at Boone's house with his brother hanging around.

At this time of night, the drive only took her about twenty minutes, Dolphin's Gate being several miles past her own development.

Slowing as she approached the guard house, Phoebe waved to the man on duty.

He nodded. "Miss Grant."

His normally friendly expression was sober, because of Audra, of course, and he waved her through. Since she'd been keeping an eye on the condo during the off-season for years, most of the guards knew her by sight and didn't need to check the windshield sticker.

Dolphin's Gate was a large enclave overlooking the bay—hence the name—and its condos, townhouses and single-family homes were all wrapped around an

eighteen-hole golf course. Not that either her mother
or her stepfather actually played golf. The prestige of
the place with its exclusive club had been the deciding factor for them.

Phoebe drove the winding road along grounds that
were lushly landscaped and manicured to perfection.
A dazzling setting if not as appealing to her as a more
natural one—like the pond she could watch by the
hour from her own lanai. There vegetation grew semi-
wild and helped provide sanctuary to scores of small
animals, birds and even an alligator or two.

Leaving the car in the drive, Phoebe entered the
townhouse. Designed by an award-winning architect
and decorated by a pricey firm, the place had always
left her cold. Nothing inside had been meant to con-
vey the feeling of warmth. Of someone actually living
there. Rather, it looked like a model, or perhaps something out of a magazine layout.

Phoebe turned on the lights and checked around the
open living area.

The ceramic backsplash in the kitchen still wasn't
complete. She'd have to contact Jimmy Bob Dortch,
see if she could light a fire under the handyman who'd
been dragging out the small job even longer than the
work he'd done for the restaurant.

Other than the tools and tiles set on a counter, not
an item seemed to be out of place. Her mother's
cleaning woman had been thorough.

Only the other day the townhouse had been in use,
two of the three bedrooms occupied by her mother
and two younger sisters, who'd flown in for the funeral. Her sisters had bunked together, avoiding the

room Audra had been living in. All three had allowed themselves what they considered an appropriate amount of grief for Audra that night, then had taken themselves back to their own lives on early flights the very next morning.

Michelle had three small kids to care for, and Janice an errant boyfriend whom she didn't trust as far as she could throw him. Phoebe had never been close to either of the younger girls, anyway, so she'd had no expectations of them. But her mother's leaving so soon had hurt.

Unknowing or uncaring that her daughter had needed her, her mother had said, *Harry wouldn't know what to do without me, poor man, not even for another day.*

And before Harry, neither had Peter nor Russell nor Stanley. Phoebe guessed her own father and Audra's had received the same single-minded attention while her mother was still married to each of them.

As Phoebe climbed the stairs to the bedrooms, she thought about her mother's choices.

Six husbands in thirty-some years. Four daughters, all with different fathers. A life of uncertainty, picking up and moving, starting over and over and over again. And all in the name of "love."

Why couldn't her mother have taken her relationships for what they were and left them at that? Why did she have to marry every man she lusted after, turning her daughters' lives into chaos?

And why was *she* wasting time bemoaning what she couldn't control? Phoebe wondered.

Irritated with herself, she entered Audra's bedroom,

as tidy as the rest of the house—far neater than Phoebe had ever seen it since Audra moved in. The cleaning woman's work, of course.

Going through drawers, inspecting her sister's effects, she tried to remain detached. One of the little things was her undoing. Her eyes filled with tears when she found the locket she'd given Audra for her sixteenth birthday. She read the inscription on the back, then opened it and stared at their pictures inside. She hadn't even known Audra had kept the cheap trinket, so at odds with the rest of her fine jewelry.

Growing up, they'd been so close. Had rarely even argued. Always made up right after. The only time Audra had stayed angry with her was over the diary. Deciding to see what all the secrecy was about, she'd been shocked by the details of her sister's intimate relationship with the boy she professed to love.

Even at fourteen, Audra had let ''love'' rule her life.

Just like their mother.

After that, Audra hid the diary so well that Phoebe couldn't find it, although not for lack of trying.

The diary...*hidden*...

Had to be hidden cleverly or the police would have found it. Phoebe had no doubt the diary would have been confiscated. Then some stranger would have paged through Audra's most personal thoughts.

Perhaps her sister hadn't brought the thing to Boone's house, after all, Phoebe decided. Too chancy that he might have gotten nosy.

Phoebe searched the bedroom and bath. Took apart the closet. No diary. No unusual hiding place. She headed downstairs. While Audra hadn't used the open living area much, she had liked the coziness of Harry's den.

They'd watched a few movies together there, had shared a few glasses of wine. Flipping on the room light, she pictured Audra on the cushy sofa, bare feet snuggled under a small throw she'd taken from the storage area inside a nearby hassock.

As always, Phoebe had automatically started straightening the room. She'd folded up the throw and had tried putting it away, but her sister had stopped her, had insisted on doing it herself. Audra, the messy one, who'd always been glad to leave the cleaning up to others.

Even then, Phoebe had thought it odd.

Pulse threading unevenly, she lifted the hassock's lid and dug down beneath several throws and small pillows. Her fingers touching the object at the bottom lifted her spirits.

With a cry of triumph, Phoebe pulled the elusive diary from its hiding place.

The knowledge was instant and didn't need to be communicated verbally. One look into each other's eyes and we knew we wanted each other.

What matter that we'd just met?

He has the sexiest dark eyes…bedroom eyes…and they told me everything I wanted to know. An excitement I've never known before curled deep inside me.

We pretended friendliness, nothing more, and left the Blue Crab separately.

No one had the faintest idea…

The entire drive home, my belly quivered with anticipation and my breasts ached for his touch. I could think of nothing else.

He was waiting for me even as I knew he would be. I didn't ask how he got past the guard. That he had and I didn't know how made it more exciting. I felt breathless, as if this would be the very first time…

We didn't make it across the living room to the stairs. Oh, how shocked mother would be that we dared abuse her new Berber carpeting as we did.

He didn't even bother taking off my clothes. Merely reached under my dress and ripped my panties free. I've never been so excited. I was already wet for him, and his fingers easily slid inside me…

"Oh, boy…"

Deciding she'd had enough titillation for one night, Phoebe rose from her bed. She was wet herself—despite the air conditioning, beads of perspiration were rolling down her back and between her breasts. Thank goodness she'd waited until she arrived home to crack open the diary, an accounting that began with the passage she'd read.

As if Audra had started a new journal to celebrate the beginning of a new life.

"Whew! What a celebration," she muttered softly, the heat pulsing from within making her distinctly uncomfortable.

A swim would cool her off.

She'd had the house built to curve around the pool. The tall sliding glass doors of the bedroom, eating nook and living area kept the humidity out and the air conditioning in during the hot months. In winter, the whole house would be open to the outside.

Undressing quickly, leaving her clothes where they fell, she snapped off the bedroom light and slid out onto the lanai, remembering the night she'd introduced them to each other. Boone had been a fairly regular customer and her sister had come around for company.

She hadn't suspected, not then.

The midnight moon silvered her surroundings as she paused at the edge of the pool and tuned in to the night. Lively splashes. Insects humming. A glimpse of a wild rabbit. Tiny geckos racing along the screened walls. All mesmerized her.

She'd been mesmerized by the passage she'd read, as well.

One look into each other's eyes and we knew we wanted each other. What matter that we'd just met? He has the sexiest dark eyes…bedroom eyes…

That particular reference had set her imagination racing.

I've never been so excited. I was already wet for him, and his fingers easily slid inside me…

In her mind, she'd seen Boone for an instant…but he'd quickly been replaced by Simon.

"Enough."

Arching, she flew into the pool without reservation, giving herself over to the water completely. She swam lengths, gracefully turning at the tiled walls without breaking her rhythm. It didn't take much to run out of steam tonight. Tension released, imagination under control, she drifted to a stop and allowed her body to hang suspended in the middle of the pool.

It was only then—when she had exhausted herself and freed her mind of the diary's seduction—that she heard a rustle behind her. Thinking a lizard or snake had found its way into the screened area, she whipped around, her gaze going straight for whatever danger lurked in the garden area at the far end of the pool.

Before she could focus, a smooth, mocking voice set her straight on the nature of her uninvited guest.

"Was that as good for you as it was for me?"

Chapter Three

Phoebe flipped back, sank and swallowed a mouthful of pool water. Thrashing to the surface, she sputtered, "What...how did you get in? And when?"

Simon Calderon stepped into a patch of moonlight. "Keys," he said, shaking what undoubtedly were the ones she'd given Audra. "About an hour ago."

"You were here when I got home? Why didn't you announce yourself then?"

He indicated the garden area. "I was waiting for you over there. Must've dropped off. Nice digs. Comfortable lounge chair."

He'd been there while she'd sprawled across her bed and read Audra's diary. While—believing she was alone—she'd stripped to the buff and had worked off the tension the passage had awakened in her.

Had he been asleep then?

Horribly embarrassed, praying the dark had shielded her from those bedroom eyes, Phoebe didn't really want to know for certain.

She did ask, "What's on your mind, Mr. Calderon?"

"Simon." He stepped closer to the pool. "And I'd be a lot more comfortable discussing it on an even plane. You want to come out or should I join you?"

Good Lord, she was buck naked, and while he couldn't see details by moonlight, he might be able to make out that much. She doubted that he'd brought a suit. The last thing in the world she needed was an in-the-buff frolic with a man whose image she hadn't been able to excise.

"Uh, I'll come out, only…I need, uh…"

"What?"

"A towel. They're on the rack over there," she said, pointing.

The moment Simon turned to fetch one, Phoebe shot forward to the pool's edge in hopes of preserving as much modesty as possible. He was back in a flash.

"Here you go."

Taking the beach towel, she dragged it into the pool. "Thanks."

"Don't you normally get out of the water before drying yourself off?"

"Gee, I never thought of that," she said stiffly.

Since he had to know she wasn't wearing a suit, Phoebe figured he was doing his best to bait her. The waterlogged terrycloth was difficult to control—it kept insisting on floating—but she managed to ascend the steps at the shallow end, dignity intact.

"You can wait out here or in the living room, if you like. I'll only be a few minutes."

"Need some help?"

The dare behind the words nearly took her breath away. "I'll manage," she choked out.

What she managed was to run trails of water over her bedroom carpeting all the way into her bathroom. Locking the door behind her, she traded the wet towel for a dry one. A brisk rub rid her of the gooseflesh that always accompanied a night swim, even in deep summer. She slipped into a loose nightshirt with an alligator design that circled her body, then quickly wrapped a dry towel around her head. Even so, her dripping had left wet streaks in the soft cotton.

Barefoot, she cautiously left her bathroom, half expecting the nervy Simon to have made himself at home on her bed. That went to show where her head was, especially since the bed remained inviolate except for the diary. Hurriedly, she snatched the leather-bound journal from the comforter and slipped it into her nightstand drawer.

Through the glass doors, she could see the lights on in the living room. Thank goodness. Maybe Simon Calderon had tired of his games and she could find out exactly what he wanted of her.

SIMON'S NERVES were on edge as he waited for Phoebe to emerge from her bedroom. He'd awakened in time to see her poised at the edge of the pool, her slender limbs clothed in nothing but moonlight. She'd caught him in a vulnerable moment…affected, he'd responded with his usual tact.

Who would blame her if she read him the riot act and showed him the door?

And now that he'd made up his mind to determine the truth about Boone—about himself—he needed her cooperation.

"Can I get you something to drink?"

Startled from his thoughts, he turned toward Phoebe's voice. She hesitated near the kitchen area.

"Soda...bottled water...juice?"

"Nothing."

As she made for the hibiscus-print chair opposite him, Simon tracked the path of the alligator wrapping itself around her damp body. The cloth clung to her bottom, molding it perfectly. As she bent over to fluff a cushion, his groin tightened, and he forced himself to look away.

A plastic alligator crouched in the base of a potted ficus near the sliding glass doors seemed to be staring at him through beady little eyes. The hand-carved wooden alligator slithering along her coffee table had him in its crosshairs. And a sketched alligator hanging over the fireplace glared down at him with something like animosity.

Of course, he only imagined their disapproval, Simon told himself.

Other creatures native to Florida—birds and reptiles and mammals—peered out from every nook and cranny, as well, giving him the oddest feeling that he was surrounded.

"I assume there's a point to your being here," Phoebe said.

He returned his attention to her. "I've had time to think."

"About?"

"The assumption that my brother was responsible for his and your sister's deaths."

Her eyebrows shot up. "I thought you agreed with the authorities."

"I did. Maybe I still do. Maybe my thinking you could be right is a stretch."

Phoebe stared at him, her thick-lashed hazel eyes wide. Another wild creature determining his worth? Simon shifted on the couch and wondered at his own reaction. Few things had the power to make him uncomfortable.

Retaliating, he absorbed every detail of her angular face, from the mole at the corner of her left eye, down her straight nose to the surprisingly soft curve of her lower lip. The towel wrapped around her head framed distinctive features that suddenly pulled into a disquieted expression...as if she fathomed his intent.

"What is it you want from me?" she finally asked, voice cool.

With the damp material of her cover-up clinging to her graceful limbs, molding to her modest breasts, provoking a hunger he hadn't fed in a while, Simon could think of a few things that had nothing to do with family...

What he said was "A truce."

"I didn't know we were at war."

"Perhaps you weren't." And the war within himself was nothing new. "But I wasn't exactly gracious last night."

"No."

"What you see is what you get." He wasn't being defensive. Merely truthful. "But if you know that going in—"

"Going in to what?" she demanded, exasperation now coloring her tone.

"Partnership."

"I have a partner."

Wondering if she meant business or personal—and what concern that was of his, he couldn't say—Simon clarified. "I meant digging for the truth."

Expression distinctly suspicious, she asked, "You want to help me?"

"Something like that."

He was thinking more of *her* helping *him,* but putting it that way might get her back up. If he'd expected her to jump for joy—for a relieved smile to erase the distrust—he would have been sorely disappointed.

"Why the sudden change of heart?" she murmured, as if she were questioning herself rather than him. "This from a man who doesn't care what other people think. Isn't that what you told me last night?"

"I'm not doing this for other people." When she still withheld any positive response, he promptly shifted gears. "Two heads are better than one, right? And I have access to Boone's business—"

"Which is important...why?"

"Maybe it's nothing more important than another source of information," he admitted. "One of the employees might have seen or heard something vital to the situation. My point is, together we can play all the angles."

"Play..." she echoed softly. "Simon, this isn't a game to me."

"Nor to me, Phoebe."

Finally, caution still shadowing her eyes, she nodded. "All right. Together, then."

He figured she'd made a concession she found somewhat disagreeable. And how could he blame her? He didn't make nice. Didn't play by the rules. Wouldn't pretend—or change to fit in—like his brother had.

Not wanting to lose the opening he'd gained, he asked, "Tell me about your sister's husband."

"Vance Laughlin," Phoebe began in a neutral tone. "Well-to-do Fort Myers businessman. Financial adviser." She took a breath. "Control freak." And allowed animosity to creep into her voice. "He likes showing off what his money can buy. That included Audra."

Wanting a true picture of the relationship, Simon knew he might be stepping into quicksand when he asked, "She married him for his money?"

Rather than being outraged, Phoebe shifted in her chair and cleared her throat. "I think the money was more of a side benefit than the real reason. Audra always went for a certain type of man. Power was her aphrodisiac. Too bad she had to go and marry it."

"That didn't make her unique by any means."

"But she was misguided, at least where it came to Vance Laughlin. I remember a time when she thought his overprotective act was romantic."

"And you have something against romance?" Simon didn't know why he'd asked the question, nor why he was so interested in Phoebe's answer.

"Not the ideal. Just the reality. Just when it makes women foolish."

He wondered if she'd ever allowed herself to be foolish where a man was concerned. Or was all her "experience" secondhand?

"At first, Audra was flattered that Vance wanted to know where she was at all times," Phoebe went on. "That he called and checked up on her, no matter where she went. But his possessiveness got old fast. She tried telling him so. The more she fought it, the more he insisted. Eventually, insistence turned to accusation."

"Another man?"

"He was certain of it."

"How about you?"

"Frankly, I'm not sure. But if there was someone, he couldn't have been important. Audra always told me about the important ones."

"Like Boone?"

"Eventually."

Her response made him think that, at least in the beginning, Boone and Audra had kept their relationship secret...undoubtedly because of Laughlin. Audra must have feared his reprisal.

"The final straw in the marriage—what was it?"

"Audra told me she felt like someone was following her. She faced Vance, asked him directly about it. He laughed, said she was imagining things. But the feeling didn't stop. Eventually, she ran scared. But even with divorce proceedings under way, she didn't feel safe. She swore she kept seeing familiar vehicles...familiar faces..."

"Was she actually being followed?"

Phoebe shrugged. "My sister did have an active

imagination...and yet...I wouldn't put anything past her husband.''

Obviously not, if she thought him capable of murder. "Maybe we ought to find out for sure."

"How?"

"From Laughlin himself."

"Oh, right, we'll just ask and he'll tell us everything we want to know."

"That's not what I meant."

"Then what?"

"I'll think of a way," he promised. "In the meantime, we shouldn't close our eyes to other possibilities. Can you think of anyone else in their lives who might have had a motive for murder?"

She seemed surprised. "If this was a crime of passion as the authorities believe, Vance is the perfect candidate."

"What about Elise Navarro?"

"Boone's assistant? What about her?"

"She took one look at me and made an up-close-and-personal acquaintance with the office floor. It made me think—"

"That a woman could have done this?"

"Murder is an equal-opportunity compulsion."

"But one that women rarely act on. And if so, then Blair Ratcliff is a more likely candidate." When he shrugged because the name rang no bells with him, she clarified. "Your brother's ex-fiancée."

Now, why should that surprise him?

"How ex?"

"Oh, about two weeks after Boone met my sister."

A woman scorned. If not two. He wasn't leaving Elise out of the equation.

"I'm telling you it was Vance."

"Maybe so." She certainly was convinced of it. "But did Audra have any more skeletons in her closet?"

With obvious reluctance, Phoebe said, "Her share."

"And maybe we should do inventory."

"She was married to Vance for nearly three years. Those skeletons were old."

"Unless she did have a lover on the side."

"I told you—"

"He couldn't have been important, because you didn't know about him."

"Good memory."

"False assumption," he countered. "If Audra did have an affair she considered meaningless, who's to say what the man's take was?"

"You're reaching."

"And I'll keep reaching until I've exhausted every possibility."

Otherwise, why bother at all? If he didn't do it right, he might as well crawl back into his swamp.

"Fine," she murmured, rising. "Speaking of exhausted…"

Getting to his feet, as well, Simon couldn't resist. "Bedtime?"

"Sleep time."

"Pity."

Though he could tell he'd flustered her, she cov-

ered well, asking, "What's our next step?" while
leading him to the front door.

"Why don't we leave that till morning. Over
breakfast. You make the coffee. I'll bring the doughnuts."

"What if I don't like doughnuts?"

"Name your poison."

"Thanks, but I'll pass. And before you leave…"
She held out her hand. "I'll take the keys. You
know…the ones you used to get inside."

She was spitting his own words from the night before back at him—so he added the phrase she'd left
out. "Or you could get them for yourself." He even
held his hands away from his pockets.

Phoebe crossed her arms and glared.

Simon was tempted to withhold them just to see
what she would do. A fleeting thought. He needed her
trust if he was to have her cooperation. Fishing the
ring out of his pocket, he dangled the keys before her
and, as she snatched them from him, noted her pal-
pable relief.

How naive.

As far as Simon was concerned, if he wanted inside
bad enough, a lock would be a mere inconvenience.

PHOEBE REMAINED near the door for several minutes
after Simon's departure. Keys digging into her palm,
she waited. Listened. When no vehicle engine started
up, her curiosity got the better of her.

How far had he come on foot?

She opened the door and stepped under the portico,
knowing it to be a futile gesture. Even with the moon

silvering the landscape, she could barely make out more than her immediate surroundings—several homes bordering the pond, a sizeable old banyan tree dominating the opposite side of the road, a stand of untouched cypress crowding the environs beyond.

With her housing development still in its infant stages, the grounds remained more natural than cultivated. There were no such things as streetlights, thank goodness.

Though even if there were, Phoebe doubted she would spot Simon Calderon if he chose not to be seen.

She imagined him as one with the wilderness he called home. Able to adapt to any condition. Masterful at blending with his environment, whether mangroves, grassland or hammock.

A feral being despite his predilection for sharp barbs...

A thought that sent a shiver along Phoebe's spine.

Hating the ease with which Simon could make her uncomfortable, she was underwhelmed by the sudden change of heart that had prompted him to stay and give her theory a try. Part of her wished he would disappear back into his swamp. But the more practical part knew she needed his help.

Bravado was all well and good, but it didn't necessarily get the job done, and no matter how much she wanted to, she wasn't certain that she *could* prove Audra and Boone had been murdered working by herself. But with Simon's cooperation, anything was possible.

Would he cooperate, though, or was he playing her for a fool?

She gazed out into nothingness, imagining he was there somewhere, watching her. She could practically feel the power of his bedroom eyes…

Another shiver.

Phoebe rubbed the raised flesh from her arms. One final glance around and she withdrew, carefully locking herself inside. Staring at the keys she'd demanded from Simon, she wondered how long a mere lock would deter him…

The adrenaline that had kept her going quickly dissipating, she turned out the lights and checked the sliding doors on the way to her bedroom. There she retrieved the diary from her nightstand drawer. Rather than picking up reading where she'd left off, however, she stared at the leather cover, traced the embossed ibis pattern with a fingertip, wondered at the power of Audra's memories.

A certain danger lay in these pages. At least for her.

The hour was too late…her imagination too vivid…her real-life encounter with Simon too fresh in her mind.

Safer readir g for the light of day, Phoebe decided, setting the diary aside until morning.

HAVING LEFT HIS PICKUP near a crushed-shell road outside Phoebe's development, Simon tangled with an overgrown cypress grove, waded through a shallow water hole and hopped a chain-link fence that wouldn't keep a trespasser—much less an experienced thief—off the property.

Safety was only an illusion.

He had thought himself safe in his seclusion, allowing the "real world" to intrude just enough to make a decent living. But the real world had come crashing in on him with a vengeance.

First his brother's death.

Now Phoebe Grant.

He found he couldn't stop thinking about the woman, even when he tried. Normally able to shut himself off from whatever he wished, his failure in this regard left him with a certain unease.

Thoughts of Phoebe, of her rushing headlong into danger, plagued him all the way back to Marco.

Once in his brother's house, however, Simon tried distracting himself from concern for the woman by going through Boone's effects…as *she* had planned to do the night before.

What had Phoebe expected to find?

Hour after hour he sought some illumination while waiting for sleep to beckon. It was as if he believed he could read his brother's thoughts by touching his things. By osmosis.

Too bad it didn't work that way.

Things were things. They had no life to give him.

Finished with the master suite, he went down to Boone's home office, began to search, tried to keep Phoebe's image from crowding his mind.

He found himself more attracted to her than was comfortable…even as his twin had been attracted to her sister?

Another link to Boone.

Alike. Too alike? Two peas in a pod...

His fingers hit something odd in the back recesses of a desk drawer. Something metal. Round. Mounted with a stone. Withdrawing it, he stared at what should have been a token of undying love.

He prayed they would find the answers that Phoebe expected. Did he hold a key in his hand?

The diamond winked at him, conspiratorial in its silence.

If the search for truth came full circle...if Boone were guilty...if *he* was destined to repeat his twin's mistakes...

It was a possibility he refused to consider.

Chapter Four

"Jimmy Bob, we've had this conversation before," Phoebe said, wearing her most serious expression.

"Yes, ma'am."

"And you promised you'd get right on it."

Tufts of light brown hair stood out around the handyman's receding hairline as he crushed his billed cap to his chest. Fortyish and built like a bull, Jimmy Bob Dortch appeared immature and defenseless, more like an embarrassed kid than a man who ran his own business.

So to speak.

"Didn't feel right," Jimmy Bob drawled. "Me goin' and workin' on your folks' place with what happened to Miss Audra and all."

Of course they'd had their last little talk more than a week before Audra's murder, but Phoebe knew she'd have to go along with his program if she was to get anywhere.

"I appreciate your sensitivity."

Not that sensitivity would get the work done. She'd called him at the crack of dawn, and he'd argued he couldn't make it into Naples that morning since he had a job on Marco, so Phoebe had quickly switched gears and said they could meet at the Blue Crab.

"Miss Audra...she was always real nice to me. Even made me a sandwich one time when I forgot my lunch."

Touched by his sad tone, Phoebe said, "My sister was a very nice person."

"And so pretty."

"That, too."

"She shouldn'ta had to die like that. Shoulda stayed away from that Calderon guy!"

Startled by his sudden intensity, by the glitter in his watery blue eyes as he muttered to himself, Phoebe caught her breath. Jimmy Bob had been in and out of the condo over a period of weeks. He must have seen Audra and Boone together sometime. Might have heard private conversations.

Did the handyman know something that might give her a clue about her sister's death?

"What do you mean—Audra should have stayed away from Boone Calderon?"

Jimmy Bob started, as if remembering he wasn't alone. "Nothin'!" he said, his face going florid. But he was crushing his cap between white-knuckled fingers. "Just that she's dead now. The police *said* it's that man's fault!"

"Sometimes the police are wrong."

The handyman was shaking his head and backing off. "Gotta go, now."

"Wait!" Phoebe cried. Then sensing he was about

to panic, she asked, "The backsplash—when can you finish?"

He was looking everywhere but at her when he said, "Right away, Miss Phoebe."

Weird was the only way to describe his reaction...as if he were afraid she might blame *him* for something. She had a feeling poking at whatever was bothering him would only make things worse. And undoubtedly she was projecting about his knowing something anyway.

In an attempt to settle him down, she asked, "What time can I expect you at Dolphin's Gate?" in as natural a tone as she could manage.

Not that she needed to be there. The security office would let him in and lock up after him. She merely wanted him to commit himself.

"Well, today I gotta finish that painting job I told you about over to Roberts Bay." He met her gaze, the panic she'd seen a moment before gone. "But I'll be right on it first thing tomorrow."

"What time?" she asked doggedly.

"Say, ten?"

"Say eight."

"Yes, ma'am."

Phoebe sighed. More than likely, Jimmy Bob would arrive whenever he pleased. But there was only so much she could do to pressure him. And, after all, he'd done a creditable job updating the bathrooms at the Blue Crab. Kevin had handled the details, so she wasn't certain if Jimmy Bob really was unreliable or merely unresponsive to *her*.

The handyman had skedaddled and she was filling

salt shakers to stall returning home and the probable confrontation with Simon Calderon, when her partner left his apartment above the restaurant. Letting the door slam behind him, Kevin took a swig of coffee and sauntered down the steps. He was barefoot and wearing a pair of disreputable cutoffs and a rumpled T-shirt that said Bang Me, Baby. His hair was sleep-tousled, and his eyes were hidden behind Ray-Bans.

"What's all the ruckus?" he grumbled as he joined her near the waitperson station.

"You're alone?" she returned. "Or is the blonde still keeping your bed warm?"

A long swallow of coffee was followed by a grin. "Hmm, interested in details, are you?"

"Forget I asked."

"She left at daybreak so she could get some sleep. What are you doing here?" He hopped onto a nearby table. "I thought you were taking the day off."

"I am. I'm only here because Jimmy Bob and I needed to have a heart-to-heart about that backsplash he's been installing in mother's kitchen."

"Wasn't he supposed to have finished already?"

"Uh-huh," she murmured, not wanting to get into it.

Kevin had sort of pushed Jimmy Bob on her, saying the poor guy needed the work. He'd no doubt feel responsible if the job weren't done right.

"You never said he wasn't getting the work done."

"I've had a few other things on my mind lately," she reminded him, topping off the last salt shaker. "I totally forgot about it."

"Dortch is a little slow."

"No kidding."

"Up here, I mean." He tapped his forehead.

"No wonder he was acting a little strange."

"Hey, he's okay working with his hands or I wouldn't have suggested you use him. I'll talk to him."

"I already did." She tried to reassure him. "Look, no big deal. I didn't even notice the job wasn't done until last night."

That seemed to take Kevin by surprise. He lifted his shades, giving her a gander at his puffy morning eyes and the furrow cutting a swath between his brows.

"You went to Dolphin's Gate instead of home? What for?"

Feeling as if she was defending herself, Phoebe said, "Looking for answers."

That morning, her hopes high, she'd flipped through Audra's diary, but it had been like searching for a needle in a haystack. Finding the kind of details that would be helpful would take some time and concentration. And the thought of meeting Simon after another dip in her sister's erotic prose, had made her put off the task again.

"Find any?" Kevin asked, cutting into her thoughts.

"What?"

"*Answers.*"

"I'm not sure."

His mouth pulled into a grim line. "Want to fill me in?"

Not on the diary, certainly.

"Simon Calderon was waiting for me when I got home."

Not on the details, either.

"Are congratulations in order?"

"Excuse me?"

"You know, that stress-relief undertaking we discussed yesterday."

Ignoring the reference to her love life, Phoebe said, "Simon decided he wants to know whether or not Boone was capable of murder, after all."

Kevin shook his head and clucked. "He's only going to encourage you."

"He's going to do more than that. He's going to help me."

"How?"

"We haven't worked out the details."

He gave her a long look before saying, "Keep me informed, would you?"

"Sure. Of course."

Though, if last night was any indication, her reports would probably have to be edited...

Before Kevin could pressure her further, Phoebe grabbed her shoulder bag. "Well, if I want the day off, I should get out of here."

"So, go," he said, though without his customary animation.

And the way he was staring at her made Phoebe uncomfortable. This wasn't like him. No grin. No wisecrack. Obviously, Kevin was worried about her, which made her feel a little guilty at leaving him out of the loop at all.

But the sight that awaited her in the parking lot

shoved all other concerns from mind. Simon Calderon was slouched in the passenger seat of her convertible.

Pulse surging, Phoebe moved toward the car. While she could see Simon's eyes were closed, she was certain he was awake and aware of her approach. She stopped beside the driver's door, and arms crossed, stared in silence until he acknowledged her presence by meeting her gaze.

Then she attacked. "How did you know where to find me?"

"And here I thought you'd be impressed."

"Did you follow me..." She took a quick glance around the parking lot but spotted no vehicle other than Kevin's. "...or did you hide in my trunk?"

"Try option C—deductive reasoning. If you weren't at home, work was the next logical place to find you."

Only she hadn't told him about the Blue Crab...

As Phoebe slid behind the wheel, the smell of doughnuts hit her. A glance over her shoulder revealed a box perched in the middle of the back seat.

He said, "We'll have to stop for that coffee since you fell down on your end."

"I told you I'd pass."

"Then we'll have to get *me* coffee."

In the end, she caved. She couldn't resist fresh doughnuts any more than the next woman.

Two purchased giant coffees and a five-minute drive later, they pulled into the Tigertail Beach lot. Simon took charge of the midmorning refreshments, while Phoebe dug into the trunk where she kept an old blanket handy for impromptu Gulf swims or picnics.

Shellers had beat them to the beach. The fanatics would have been out there before dawn, but even at this hour, a considerable number of people strolled the tide line, stooping and sifting through the wash for whelks and buttercups, scotch bonnets and jewel boxes, cockles and olive shells. Others had waded through the thigh-high water to get to the sandbar that acted as a natural breakwater.

A flock of gulls looking for handouts dive-bombed a couple of tourists holding up French fries, while a reddish egret stumbled like a drunk in the shallows—activity designed to confuse its prey.

Sighing with pleasure, Phoebe raised her face to the sun and tilted her head so the breeze rippled through her loose hair. An hour from now, heat would blast the open area, but for the moment, it was heaven.

Even Simon seemed relaxed as gulls gathered around them, waiting for a sweet treat. He lay back on one elbow, handsome-as-sin face out to sea... throat long and tanned...jaw freshly shaved, scar more visible than before...ruffled hair teasing his forehead.

For once, he actually appeared unthreatening.

Possibly accessible.

Yet Phoebe waited until she'd devoured three doughnuts and had washed them down with the better part of her coffee before asking, "So, did you figure out how to approach my brother-in-law?"

"I have a few ideas." He sat up, suddenly all business. "To start, might Audra have left a few things behind?"

"Almost everything," Phoebe said. "She just wanted out."

"Then give him a call and tell him you'd like to go through Audra's things."

"What makes you imagine he'll agree? He's not a fan of mine any more than I am of his."

"So play emotional. Distraught. Helpless. A burden on his back who isn't going away until she gets what she wants. Tell him you need something to remember Audra by. Something...that was special to you."

Thinking of the locket she'd already found, Phoebe figured she could use that as an excuse. Vance wouldn't keep track of something so insignificant as a cheap trinket. It could be anywhere for all he knew.

"I can try," she said.

"Do better than try. Get him to agree."

"Then what?"

"Does he have domestic help?"

"Audra had a woman come in twice a week to clean...I can't imagine Vance would have chosen to take over her duties himself."

"Then you arrange to get in when she's there. Once *you're* in, *I'm* in. Get the picture?"

"Crystal clear." Wondering if that would consti tute illegal entry, Phoebe said, "You have more confidence in this plan than I do."

"Do you want to prove someone other than Boone pulled the trigger or not?"

His irritation startled her. "You know I do."

"Did you think it would be easy?" he asked. "Or safe?"

Safe? With him?

Phoebe knew that's not what he meant. If they *did* stumble on some truths a murderer was trying to hide...

The conclusion stole her breath away.

"No, but I—didn't have time to think things through."

"If we don't go into this with complete confidence, what's the use?"

Knowing Simon had a point didn't make Phoebe feel better, however. Her stomach swirled as if she'd swallowed a couple of live snakes. She was starting to regret the doughnuts.

"I could use a walk," she muttered, getting up and heading for the water.

Her world suddenly narrowed, the sights and sounds around her shifting out of focus.

Simon joined her, choosing to stay dry while she strolled in the shallows. She took deep calming breaths and let waves wash over her feet. The smooth rolling motion of the water had a calming effect on her system.

"Better," she murmured.

"Keep in mind you're not alone in this anymore."

"Safety in numbers? You have to be kidding. Two can die as easily as one. I'd suggest you ask Audra and Boone...if they weren't already dead."

"Maybe they didn't see it coming."

"And we will?"

"I'll be watching for it, and if you're real smart, you will, too."

Simon slipped his hand around hers and gave it an encouraging squeeze. Phoebe's pulse jumped. She was hoping he didn't notice.

That she was attracted to him was undeniable.

That he was all wrong for her equally so.

She made it a rule to keep her relationships uncomplicated if physically satisfying and to end them cleanly before anyone got hurt.

There was nothing uncomplicated about Simon Calderon. Intense...brooding...overwhelming. He could be all of those. Not the type to let her call the shots, or to let something end before *he* deemed it over. In the end, *she* would be the one who got hurt.

She *wouldn't* let that happen—wouldn't follow in her mother's footsteps.

Nor in Audra's.

And yet disappointment warred with relief when Simon stopped and released her hand.

He said, "I found something interesting last night." Then reached into his shirt pocket, from which he produced what was obviously an engagement ring. A very expensive one, to judge by the unusual platinum setting and the size of the diamond. He handed it to her. "Recognize this?"

"Should I?"

"Read the inscription."

She maneuvered the thick band until she could focus on the single word etched inside: *Forever*.

A lump settled in her throat, making it difficult to ask, "You think Boone had this made up for Audra?"

"Doubtful. I found it thrown to the back of a desk drawer like it didn't matter for anything."

"Blair, then?"

"That would be my take."

Remembering the haughty society beauty's manner, Phoebe said, "Blair didn't take rejection well. She told people the breakup was her idea, that Boone had never been good enough for her and that she'd finally realized it. I'm surprised she returned the ring."

"If Boone gave it to her in the first place. Do you remember her wearing one?"

She shook her head. "I only met her a couple of times at the Blue Crab. I don't usually look at women's hands for engagement rings."

"What if Boone meant to give this to Blair but met Audra first?" Speculation lent a hard edge to Simon's features. "As his brother, wouldn't it be fitting that I give it to the woman he bought it for? She might even be grateful enough to let down her guard."

"Sounds like you have a plan."

"It's a way to meet Boone's ex without putting her on notice."

"What if she won't see you?"

"She'll see me."

Phoebe believed him. If Blair Ratcliff didn't succumb to curiosity, Simon wouldn't hesitate to invite himself.

"What do you hope to gain?"

"If I'm lucky, a little insight into her nature."

"We have a start, then. You have your assignment and I have mine."

Which meant she'd have the opportunity to delve into Audra's diary.

They headed back the way they'd come, picking up the blanket, refuse and—to the disgust of protesting gulls—the few remaining doughnuts.

After placing all in the trunk and slamming the lid, she realized Simon was staring at her, eyes lit with a speculative gleam.

"What?" she asked.

"You could have left me a note this morning. You knew I'd be back."

"You could have called."

"Would you have picked up?"

"Why not?"

"I make you nervous."

"Get over yourself."

Amusement played around the corners of his mouth and his bedroom gaze resurfaced. Phoebe figured getting into the car fast would be wise. But before she could make a move, Simon placed his hands on the trunk on either side of her, effectively trapping her.

Then, without warning, he kissed her.

Her heart stilled as he slipped inside her mouth as easily as he'd slipped inside her mind.

Her tongue reached out for his. When their tips touched, her heart began to race, as if playing catch up. Her every nerve, every inner fibre, every inch of skin was suddenly alive…hypersensitive…gasping for nourishment that only he could provide. A rush of hot blood coursed through her, fine-tuning all her senses until they were filled only with him.

And then Simon let go of her so suddenly that

Phoebe teetered and was glad for the car at her back. Shocked, she stared at him until her senses righted.

"What was that for?" she gasped.

"Just proving my point."

Only he wasn't smiling now...

Nor was she.

Uh-oh...

Phoebe was aghast. She'd just collided with the very thing she'd been trying her best to avoid since meeting Simon. Try as she might to forget the incident ever happened, however, she was only made of flesh and blood.

Weak flesh, she amended ruefully, unable to settle down inside. Just like the other women in her family.

Only she was the one with sense enough to label what she was feeling for exactly what it was, no more. No hearts and flowers. No pretense.

She was simply in lust with the man.

Now what was she going to do about it?

THE RATCLIFF HOME proved to be a three-story contemporary mansion set in a subtropical garden overlooking Naples Bay. A pale coral ceramic-tile roof topped tasteful white stucco. The upper two floors were surrounded by a veranda. From what Simon could tell, every room had access to the outside.

As he pressed the door buzzer, he steeled himself against another weird reaction from the person who answered. But the uniformed young woman who opened the door didn't seem to know him from Adam.

"Can I help you, sir?" she asked pleasantly.

"Simon Calderon. I'm here to see Blair Ratcliff. Is she in?"

The young woman nodded. "Please follow me."

She led him through a media room the size of a small theater and out to the largest lanai he'd ever seen. One end was dotted with full-grown palm trees whose fronds nearly reached the screened roof.

"If you'll wait, I'll alert Miss Blair."

"I'll be here."

Simon wandered through what appeared to be a living room with cushioned rattan sofas and chairs and glass-topped tables. Flanking either side of the sitting area were formal gardens set around sizable sculptures, and before him was a swimming pool with a waterfall rushing down from the hot tub above. Though outdoors, the area was made more comfortable by misters, the finely sprayed water droplets released by concealed valves overhead.

He'd barely taken in his surroundings when the door behind him opened.

A tall, curvaceous redhead wearing a flower-print dress barely more substantial than a one-piece swimsuit breezed out of the house. On seeing him, she stopped dead. Though her thick-lashed green eyes grew wide, she didn't take long to find her voice.

"I don't know why I'm even the tiniest bit surprised. He did say you were twins."

"Then you may be the only one he told."

"Not surprising," she purred, moving closer. "Boone and I had a very special relationship, until that Laughlin witch decided to leave her husband and go after him. Some women always want what they can't have."

"It seems that Audra did have Boone, however."

"Yes...well..." Her shrug was nonchalant and her classically beautiful features remained composed. "Now she has him forever, doesn't she?"

A bit cruel considering the circumstances, Simon decided, choosing to take the opening.

He echoed, "Forever," then patted down his pockets as if she'd just reminded him of something. "The reason I'm here...one of them...was to return this to you."

He whipped out the engagement ring and handed it to her, while carefully watching for her reaction.

Blair gave the valuable piece of jewelry little more than a glance before pitching it onto a side table as if it were so much junk.

"Now what were those other reasons?" she asked.

"Mainly, I wanted to meet you to say how sorry I was—"

"That Boone died? Yes, it is a shame, isn't it?" She sauntered to a drink cart. "Can I offer you a glass of wine? Something stronger?"

"Not for me, thanks. I was going to say how sorry I was that my brother broke your heart."

Her expression amused, she poured a Merlot for herself. "Do I appear to be some pitiful, broken-hearted creature?"

Actually, she appeared to be one cold cookie. Under other circumstances, Simon would have said so, without compunction. But, now, because he wanted something from her, he chose to play her carefully.

He took a seat on one of the sofas and said, "Sometimes we cover our true emotions."

"I assure you, Simon, my heart is intact. Don't get me wrong. I was quite fond of Boone—while it lasted. But I'm the one who broke off the engagement."

"And from what I understand, with good reason."

Blair claimed a chair opposite him and crossed her tanned legs, allowing her already short skirt to ride up her shapely thighs. Her feet were bare, her toenails painted the same shocking shade of orange as her long fingernails. And her ankle bracelet appeared to be a thick gold ribbon, the clasp an emerald larger than the diamond in the ring. Matching emeralds hid her earlobes.

"I could have defeated the witch at her own game," she was saying, "but I was already bored with playing and I was hanging in only because it was easier. Boone and I were well matched in the bedroom. But in the drawing room and the family business..." She shrugged. "He didn't quite measure up to Ratcliff standards, after all."

"Business?"

"Daddy is Jay Ratcliff." When he didn't respond, she clarified. "Jay Ratcliff Jewelers."

"I see," Simon said, though he didn't really.

The rich and famous held no fascination for him. But Blair's background might explain her easy contempt for the costly ring. Undoubtedly, she was accustomed to her pick of fine jewelry.

"Mamma and Daddy were furious when I started

seeing Boone. I guess our brief engagement was my way of showing them that I was my own woman.''

"You're saying you used Boone?"

A smile quirked her orange-hued lips. "We used each other, Simon. Isn't that what grown-ups do?"

A rhetorical question, one he chose not to address. "Who are you using now?" he asked instead.

Her eyebrows arched. "Interested?"

"Curious."

If Blair *had* gotten over Boone as she'd implied, surely she'd be involved with someone else by now.

"We could discuss it later," she suggested. "Say...over drinks?"

She was challenging him, no doubt about it. Why? To find out, he supposed he'd have to take the bait. Which presented him with a further opportunity to delve into her psyche, to determine if she was capable of murder. She'd already contradicted herself, first saying she and Boone had a special relationship until Audra came into the picture, then claiming she'd only been hanging in because it was easier.

"Make that dinner," he said, choosing to keep the upper hand. "Tomorrow night."

"The Wharf? It overlooks the water. Near Tin City."

"I'll find it."

"At nine."

"Seven," he countered. "I'm an early riser so I get to bed early."

"Don't worry," she murmured. "That can be arranged."

Her expression reminded Simon of a cat planning to snack on an unwary, slightly stupid mouse.

Chapter Five

Uncertainty competed with loathing as Phoebe waited for Vance Laughlin to take her call. It galled her that she had to speak to Audra's estranged husband at all. It galled her that she would have to treat the probable murderer with politeness, perhaps deference. She only hoped she would be convincing enough over the phone that she wouldn't actually have to challenge him in person.

Suddenly the line came alive with his sharp, "Yeah, what do you want, Phoebe?"

Nice greeting...not that she should have expected any better of him.

At least he wasn't pretending to be the poor, anguished widower as he had with the police and the media after the bodies were discovered. To the rest of the world, he'd been the picture of abject grief. She'd caught his act on those video clips run on the nightly news and again at the funeral and graveside. For a moment, she'd thought he was going to fling himself on the coffin.

And part of her had wanted him to…wouldn't have minded seeing him buried alive…

She took a deep breath and plunged in. "Vance, I need to talk to you about— "

"So talk already!"

"—going through Audra's personal effects." Another breath. "You know, for the family."

Silence.

Butterflies fluttering through her stomach, Phoebe clenched her jaw and waited. Simon's advice on how to handle her brother-in-law—using feminine wiles, as she saw it—didn't sit well with her. But she'd already promised herself she would do whatever was necessary.

Finally, he said, "Tell me why I should even give you the time of day."

"I was your wife's sister."

"Who tried setting the cops on me!"

Wondering how he could know, Phoebe shrank inside. "I merely answered their questions," she lied, heart hammering. "They were so thorough…wanting to know about the problems in the marriage…the spirit of the breakup. I—I was naturally upset over Audra's death. I truly don't remember everything they asked or implied."

Vance waited a beat before saying, "You already have access to Audra's things at your mother's place."

She thought he sounded calmer. Had he bought her fabrication, then? If only she knew exactly who had told him what.

"I'm certain you're aware that Audra didn't take all that much with her when she left you, Vance."

Her sister had wanted her freedom and well-being more than things. Thank goodness. That allowed Phoebe a pretext on which to get into her brother-in-law's home, and hopefully, to find something that would upset the neat theory the authorities had so readily accepted.

"What exactly do you expect to find, Phoebe?" Vance asked smoothly.

She heard the underlying distrust in his tone. To allay any suspicions he might have, she drew on Simon's advice and used a purposely shaky voice.

"I—I'm not sure. Photos…some k-keepsakes.. maybe the locket."

"I don't remember any locket."

"I'm sure she didn't w-wear it anymore. It wasn't worth anything to anyone but the two of us," Phoebe said. As she stared down at the piece of inexpensive jewelry nestled in her palm, real if unexpected tears gathered in her eyes. She didn't have to pretend to be emotional. "It was my present to Audra for her sixteenth birthday."

"What makes you think she kept the damn thing?"

"Some people are sentimental. Besides, Audra promised me she would keep it forever." Hating to grovel, she nevertheless said, "Please, Vance, just cut me some slack this one time and I won't bother you again," in a slightly whiny voice.

A longer silence.

During which all manner of thoughts flitted through Phoebe's mind, first and foremost being whether or not he was on to her. If the real killer guessed her true purpose…

Not that she could let that possibility stop her.

Then he said, "If you must," the simple words conveying his continued reluctance if not further suspicion. "You're in luck. This is one of Regina's days." He sounded cold now. All business-efficient. "I'll call the house and alert her. What time should I say you'll be there?"

"I'm not exactly sure." Phoebe didn't have a clue as to when Simon would return. "In a couple of hours, I guess. I have a few things I need to take care of first. For the Blue Crab," she added, hoping her mentioning the bar and grill would further allay his suspicions.

"Just be out of there before I get home."

"Yes, of course."

She didn't want to see Vance any more than he wanted to see her. They'd disliked each other from the get-go, she because of the type of man he was, he because of her keenness. As if he hadn't had a thing to do with the wreck of his own marriage, he'd actually blamed *her* when Audra had first left him.

And now she blamed *him* for her sister's death.

She was happy to end the conversation and even happier that her number-one suspect had unknowingly given her permission to find proof of his guilt. A thrill of anticipation shot through her.

Then came the waiting.

Fixing herself a fruit salad for lunch, Phoebe was hoping Simon would call, but no such luck. She regretted not having told him to check in with her. For all she knew, he might not be back until it was too late to get to Fort Myers, find what they needed and get out before her brother-in-law left his office. And undoubtedly hell would freeze over before Vance was so amenable again.

A quick swim worked off some of her anxiety. Changing into loose cotton pants and shirt, she checked the clock. Nearly two. Where the heck was Simon? He'd better be getting the goods on Blair Ratcliff.

Not knowing what else to do with herself until he chose to show, she faced the inevitable.

He's making life miserable for me. Won't accept that I've left him for good. That it's over. That I have no feelings for him…if I ever did.

Went for drinks with him. One last try to convince him in a civilized manner. He saw it as his chance to woo me back into his bed, into his life. When I resisted, he turned ugly, acted like he could force me if he wanted to. I told him to go to hell and got home on my own.

He doesn't care about me, really, just doesn't want to lose a trophy.

But I don't want to lose my sanity…or my life.

Besides, I have Boone now. Couldn't even think about letting another man touch me. Not that I can share that with anyone yet. Not even with Phoebe.

Keeping our relationship clandestine has its advantages. The secrecy itself is too titillating to give up. Even thinking about being with him arouses me. And when I set eyes on him, my desire feels beyond bearing....

We continue to pretend nothing more than friendliness in public, while in private anything goes.

Tonight we didn't wait to get home. I excused myself for the ladies' room. Before I could lock the door, he'd followed me inside.

What if someone figured out what we were doing?

Thinking that they might...that maybe one of them would walk in on us...added a sense of urgency...a seductive hint of danger....

This time, he took me on the edge of the sink. Didn't even bother to remove my panties, merely pushed the material aside before he slid inside me. I leaned back and wrapped my legs around his waist and set my shoulders against the mirror so he could push deeper and fill me completely.

Oh, does he know how to work me. The whispered words...that bedroom gaze....

It didn't take me long to approach the edge. Just as I was losing it, he reached behind me and hit the faucet handle, spraying my back with icy water.

I went up like a geyser....

The doorbell practically made Phoebe jump out of her skin. She fumbled with the diary and was shoving it in the bedside drawer when the chime sounded again.

"Coming!" she yelled.

Heart pumping, trying to shake the effect that left her trembling inside and feeling a little guilty besides, she somehow made her way to the front door. Throwing it open, she came face-to-face with Simon.

One look at her and he raised his eyebrows and lowered his sleepy-looking lids, as if he could tell what she'd been doing...what she was thinking.

She was imagining him pinning her up against the edge of the sink—

"Can I come in?"

"Oh. Right."

Phoebe stepped aside and he glided into the living area, his arm brushing hers. She fought the weak-kneed feeling that followed. She had to get over this. Stop thinking of him every time she read a diary entry. Keep straight in her mind that Audra's fantasies were not hers. That Boone was not Simon, no matter how much they looked alike.

"Did I catch you at a bad time?"

He'd caught her all right, Phoebe thought, closing the door. "Actually, I was just reading while I was waiting to hear from you." She wanted to tell him about the diary less than ever. "I talked Vance into letting me into the house."

"When?" Simon asked.

"We should leave right away."

All the rationalization in the world proved to be nothing but a mental exercise. Her flesh *was* weak. And deprived. Staying sharp around Simon would be a feat in itself.

Leaving him for a moment to slip on some sandals and fetch her shoulder bag gave her the space to cool down. And to remember Audra's entry: *I don't want to lose my sanity…or my life.* Surely they'd find something. Then she was all efficiency, hurrying Simon into her car, not indulging in conversation until they were on the road.

"What about you?" she finally asked. "Did you get to Blair?"

His "You could say that" held a wealth of meaning that unaccountably irritated her.

Phoebe sneaked a glance Simon's way, but sunglasses shaded his eyes, and for once he was wearing a poker face. Because Blair had gotten to him as well as his brother? Boone had once been seduced by the society beauty.

What was to say his twin didn't have a similar taste in women?

Voice clipped, she asked, "So what did you learn?"

"Just that Blair Ratcliff doesn't wear her heart on her sleeve. She's either one cold cookie or a really talented liar."

Relaxing her death grip on the steering wheel, she murmured, "I could have told you that."

"But I'll get another chance at her tomorrow night."

At her? "How so?"

"We're meeting for dinner. Her suggestion. At least the meeting part was hers."

"Why bother?" she asked lightly.

"She came on to me. It'll be interesting to see where she takes it."

Phoebe swallowed hard. Blair Ratcliff was a gorgeous woman. One she couldn't compete with. If she wanted to compete. Which she didn't.

She snapped on the radio to a raucous Spanish-language station out of Miami. Unfortunately, this was one time she couldn't get into the salsa beat. Still, she hid behind the music.

And Simon didn't try to initiate any conversation all the way into Fort Myers. When they were only a couple of miles from their destination, however, he reached over and hit the radio's power switch.

"What kind of setup does Laughlin have?"

"A big house on a few acres."

"No water access?"

"He hates boats."

"Sounds like that's lucky for us. How close is the house to the road or a neighbor?"

"More than spitting distance."

"Is there a drive?"

"A long one."

"Open?"

"Vegetation."

"What kind?"

"A hodgepodge of native plants and trees most of the way."

"Any reason I'm having to drag this information out of you?" he finally asked.

Phoebe flushed. "No, of course not." What in the world was wrong with her? "It's just that I've never done anything like this before. I guess I'm a little nervous."

"Which is understandable."

Though she wasn't certain which made her more so—their mission or Simon himself.

He gave her a moment of breathing space before saying, ''Once we're on the property, drive slow and I'll get out somewhere along the way.''

She glanced at him. ''I figured you could just duck low in the car and stay there until I signaled you that it was safe to sneak into the house.''

''And chance someone seeing me?''

''I thought the object was your getting inside.''

''It is.''

''But if I don't know where you'll be, how will I—''

''I'll find you. All you have to do is make sure a first-floor door or accessible window is unlocked.''

''Piece of cake,'' she muttered, already worrying how she was going to manage that under Regina's nose.

And how would Simon get inside without alerting the cleaning woman?

Phoebe gave him details of the house's layout, so once he was in he would know what was what. While she was going through Audra's things, as she'd told Vance—her purpose being very different from the one stated, of course—Simon would be taking her brother-in-law's study apart. She only hoped they weren't on a fool's errand.

Turning off the main road, she tried to ease her own qualms. But as they slowed before the entrance to the Laughlin property, her anxiety mounted. She gripped the steering wheel with palms that were starting to sweat.

"Stay cool," Simon said, as if he sensed her growing distress.

"I'm trying."

She made the turn and put the car in first, barely giving it enough gas to move up the drive. He was craning around, getting the lay of the land. As she'd indicated, both sides of the drive were lined with growth, low-growing sea oats giving way to strangler figs, gumbo limbo and live oak.

Not a soul was in sight.

"Tell me when."

"That curve just ahead..."

His hand went to the door handle and her foot came off the accelerator, slowing them even more. When she heard the catch release, she gently tapped the brake, urging the car to a near standstill. He flashed out of the still-rolling vehicle, slamming the door closed behind him. He made straight for the foliage on his side of the road and disappeared so quickly she might have imagined the scenario.

She put her foot back on the accelerator, but barely gave the car gas. Better to maintain a steady slow speed than rouse any suspicions, in case someone was around and tracking her movements.

A moment later, the house became visible. As always, Phoebe remained unmoved by its similarity to an old plantation manor fronted by two-story white columns. The only other car in sight was Regina's subcompact, which she'd left outside the garage. Relieved that no one else was around, she parked the convertible on the wide circular drive, which seemed designed for a carriage drawn by a team of horses.

Before Phoebe had a chance to ring the bell, the front door opened to reveal a wiry woman whose small stature disguised her strength. For once, Regina wasn't smiling. Her dark face was drawn into a sad expression.

"Mr. Laughlin said to expect you."

"Hello, Regina." Phoebe entered the house she'd hoped never to set foot in again.

"This is a sad time for you," the cleaning woman said as she closed the door. "And me. I liked Miss Audra a whole lot."

"She liked you, too."

"She was always kind to me. Respectful," Regina added. "Not like some."

Though she didn't name him, Phoebe figured the woman meant Vance. Phoebe doubted that her brother-in-law was kind or sincerely respectful toward anyone.

"Where did Mr. Laughlin store my sister's things?"

"Store? He ain't touched nothin'. Everythin's like it was when Miss Audra moved out. He even made me keep her rooms spit-and-polish clean—like he figured she was gonna come back any time."

While her sister had shared the master suite with her husband at night, Phoebe knew she'd had her own dressing room and bath, plus a dayroom downstairs.

"Well, then, I don't have to sort through boxes."

"Nope. Miss, if you want me to help you, all you gotta do is ask. You tell me what you're lookin' for and I can most probably find it for you."

If only…

"I'm not even sure what, Regina. I just want a few things to remember her by." Phoebe grew edgy. She hated lying to someone so sincere. "I really need to do this for myself, but thank you."

"I understand."

"Besides, this is a big house. I'm sure you still have a lot to do and I know how particular Mr. Laughlin can be. I wouldn't want him angry with you."

"Me, neither," the woman muttered. "I'll be getting back to the kitchen, then. Can I get you anythin'? Something cool to sip?"

"I'm fine."

Phoebe nearly collapsed with relief when Regina finally left her alone. She waited until the woman was out of sight before sneaking into the great room, where Vance's taste reigned. Instead of a light or bright decor that would go with the sunny space, he'd insisted on heavy woods, darker rugs and traditional muted upholstery patterns. The effect was funereal. And the air conditioning was set so high that Phoebe could imagine it being cold enough to store a corpse...

Audra had avoided the room whenever possible and Phoebe didn't blame her.

Able to hear faint strains of Regina's singing coming from the kitchen, she opened a set of French doors and stood fixed, trying to spot Simon. Humid heat assaulted her from the front while the room's conditioned air chilled her back. The effect was odd and disturbing, unexpectedly reminding her of Audra's water-faucet experience.

Reminding her of Simon.

Senses swimming, she felt as if his gaze had found her and those bedroom eyes were pinning her with their intensity...undressing her...

"Oh, no...!" Realizing that it was happening again, she grimaced. She had to stop this, had to concentrate on what was important. She couldn't afford to be distracted this way.

But try as she might, Phoebe couldn't tell if Simon was in position yet. Plenty of cover on this side of the house. He'd merely have to chance an open expanse of several yards.

Silently urging him to show his face, she realized he was probably just being extra cautious. All she could do was hope that he'd spotted her. She backed into the house, pulling the doors shut but leaving them unlocked. She stared through the glass.

Still seeing nothing of the man who plagued her, Phoebe finally turned toward the stairs that would take her to Audra's old dressing room.

SIMON WAITED UNTIL Phoebe disappeared inside before considering an approach to the house. His antenna raised, he sensed no threat, yet he took one last thorough look around before stepping from his camouflage and out into the sunlight.

A few seconds of exposure brought him to the French doors, which opened easily and silently. He slipped inside. Ears tuned to the most minute sound, he placed the cleaning woman somewhere off to the right.

He veered to the left.

Phoebe's description of the house's layout had been precise. Quickly finding Laughlin's office, he gazed around a room even darker and colder than the one he'd just left.

Where to begin?

From what he could see, the cleaning woman had already finished in here. Everything seemed in order.

No stacks of files on the credenza...no scraps of note paper on the desk...no Post-its attached to the computer monitor...

Simon turned to the desk calendar.

He checked over every entry made during the past several months, day by day, found nothing unusual, then checked again to be certain.

The desk drawers were equally neat. Equally uninformative.

Same with the file cabinets.

Simon knew a moment's despair. Perhaps there was nothing to find? Then he chastised himself for expecting too much, too soon. He was becoming more anxious than Phoebe.

But his stake in this was more urgent, more personal than hers. He wasn't only beginning to bet on his brother's innocence. By virtue of their oneness, and theirs was possibly the closest connection one person could have with another, he was betting on himself.

A ceiling-to-floor bookcase backed the desk. He pulled a volume free. Perfect condition, as if it hadn't ever been touched. Was Laughlin that careful, then? With all his possessions? With Audra?

Or only with those that didn't matter?

The books, too, were perfectly aligned by size and type, enough to fill each shelf from side to side. In the midst of concentrating his attention elsewhere, Simon hesitated and turned back to the book wall.

There was something out of place...

He focused on several volumes at one end of the shelf directly above eye level and immediately saw what it was that bothered him about them. They protruded a quarter of an inch forward from their neighbors.

How odd...

He hesitated barely a moment before reaching for the tomes, freeing them from their perch. His pulse quickened as their secret was revealed. They'd been hiding a large manila envelope that stood flat against the back of the bookcase.

"Well, what do we have here?" he murmured.

Simon abandoned his armload of books on the desk, not bothering to catch one that slid across its polished surface and knocked a tray of paper clips to the carpeted floor. Instead, he reached for the padded mailer that had been purposely hidden from view.

The typed label on its face gave up Vance Laughlin's name and an unfamiliar Fort Myers address. No doubt the man's office. No return information, of course. And across the packet's front, Photos: Do Not Bend was stamped in red ink.

Telling himself not to expect anything of value, Simon inspected the envelope's contents.

Which reassured him they might very well be on the right track...

OF ALL THE THINGS she might have found, Phoebe hadn't expected a second diary. One quick flip through the handwritten pages and she shoved the leather-bound journal into the bottom of her shoulder bag.

Another thing she would keep from Simon.

Her secrecy would be justified, Phoebe assured herself. If she shared this with him, he would suspect a more current chronicle existed. And unless she found some proof of Vance's guilt within its pages, she couldn't—wouldn't—share her sister's most private thoughts with anyone.

Especially not with Simon.

Because somehow, he would know.

He'd take one look at her and...

Phoebe pulled herself together.

She'd gone through the dressing room carefully but had found nothing significant before lifting the shoe box that had felt too heavy for shoes. She replaced the sandals that had topped the diary and returned the box to its shelf before checking the others.

Then finished with her search, she headed downstairs for the day room.

Having heard no untoward ruckus, she assumed Simon had gotten into Vance's study without incident. Had he found anything of significance? Tempted to check on him, she paused at the study door.

Before she could put hand to knob, however, a warning creak twirled her around to face the very man she'd been hoping to avoid. He towered over her, his gray eyes deadly cold as they pinned her to the spot.

"Vance!" Phoebe gasped.

Dear Lord, they were trapped by the murderer!

Chapter Six

Loud enough to be heard even through a thick wooden door, Phoebe said, "Oh, good grief, Vance, you startled me." Hoping to convince him, she threw a dramatic hand to her breast as if trying to still her madly pumping heart. "I really wasn't expecting to see you."

"Obviously not."

"I mean I…uh, know I was supposed be gone by the time you got home."

"I left the office early."

Purposely, no doubt.

His expression chilled Phoebe. Why hadn't Audra noticed how cruel his smile could be *before* marrying the creep? Instead, she'd been blinded by his smooth good looks, his meticulous appearance and his powerful aura.

Phoebe was certain that she hadn't tamed his suspicions, though. He'd obviously meant to catch her "in the act" all along. She'd have to outfox him. Despite the silver at his temples (evidence of the probable decade he had on Simon), he kept himself in top shape. And who was to say he wasn't carrying a gun? Either way, he could do damage to them both.

Look what he'd done to Audra and Boone...

Innocently, she murmured, "I didn't hear your car pull up," in hopes of distracting him.

He ignored her feeble attempt. "I thought maybe you needed some help."

Vance Laughlin volunteering to help *her?* Not bloody likely. She went along with his ploy, though, indicating the door several yards along.

"I was just about to see what I could find in Audra's day room."

"Funny. It looked as if you were more interested in my study." Gray eyes flat, he smoothly asked, "What did you hope to find, Phoebe?"

Her heart hammered faster. It was all she could do not to turn tail and escape to her car. But she had Simon to think of. She'd gotten him into this...

"In your study? Nothing."

Vance was already opening the door. "Why don't we see? Together."

Her heart beat its way out of her chest and into her throat where it threatened to choke her. From the corner of her eye, she caught Regina standing at the end of the hall, gaping at her. Swallowing hard, Phoebe followed Vance inside, darting her gaze from one dark corner to another.

No sign of Simon.

Had he been there at all?

Vance, too, was slowly looking around, seemingly checking over every object. Knowing how particular he was—Audra had claimed that if one item were out of place he would immediately notice—she studied him for any reaction.

For a moment, his gaze lingered on the bookshelf behind his desk...

Phoebe's gaze followed his. *What in the world had his attention?* She caught herself holding her breath.

Finally, he turned back to her. "Did you find what you were looking for?"

"What?"

He was accusing her...and she was trying to appear innocent. *Trying* being the operative word.

"That piece of jewelry you gave Audra," he said. "That's what you indicated you hoped to recover."

"Jewelry?" Phoebe echoed.

Fear was disorienting her, making her stupid. She couldn't seem to focus her thoughts.

"A locket, wasn't it?"

"Locket. Right." She shoved a hand into her pants pocket and pulled out the treasure, which, fortunately, she'd brought with her. "Here it is."

"I've never seen that before."

He grabbed the locket and chain from her hand. First he read the message inscribed on the back of the heart. Then he flicked it open with a perfectly manicured thumb nail and glanced at the aged photographs inside.

Though he remained expressionless, Phoebe would swear he was disappointed. He threw the trinket back at her. Gasping, Phoebe caught it even as the pressure released from her chest like the air out of a pricked balloon.

"Since you've found what you were looking for, you can leave," he informed her.

"But the day room—"

"Holds nothing for you." He started toward the door, then stopped. Something on the floor near the desk caught his attention. He bent at the waist. "Now how did that get there?" He quickly straightened, paper clip in hand. "You wouldn't know anything about this?"

No need to feign surprise. "A paper clip?"

"This wasn't on the floor when I left this morning."

She shrugged. "Don't look at me. This is the first I've been in your office."

"Is there anyone else in this house?"

About to deny it, she was preempted.

"Me." The cleaning woman stood in the doorway, dark eyes wide, her already thin body seeming narrower somehow. "Sorry, Mr. Laughlin. I—I knocked over the tray when I was dustin'. Musta missed pickin' up one of them critters."

Certain Regina was lying for her, Phoebe went wide-eyed herself. She hadn't been in here before. Which meant that Simon had! Considering his purpose, could he have gotten in and out so fast?

Where in the heck was he?

As Phoebe covertly peered around again, this time for some other exit, Vance said, "Very careless of you, Regina."

"Yessir."

The windows?

"See that it doesn't happen again."

"Yessir."

The windows appeared secured to her.

Anger warred with disappointment in his face as Vance spun toward Phoebe and bellowed, "As for you—"

"Consider me gone."

She whipped past Regina fast. Not fast enough to miss the satisfied quirk of the other woman's lips, though.

Regina *knew*.

Whether the cleaning woman had actually seen Simon or had merely sensed Phoebe's underlying purpose, she had no way of telling. And this was not the time to ask.

Grateful for the woman's intervention, whatever her motive, Phoebe vowed to repay her somehow.

In the meantime, where was Simon?

And where was Vance's car? Not in the drive. And Regina's car still blocked the entry to the garage.

Vance had purposely left his car away from the house, maybe on the old shell road used by tradesmen, so he wouldn't alert her.

His deviousness certainly pointed to his guilt.

Clambering behind the wheel and starting the engine, she kept an eye out for some trace of Simon as she pulled away from the house. Nothing. Again she drove slowly along the same route to the main road.

What if Simon was trapped in the house with Vance?

Phoebe prayed the man would have the sense to stay hidden for as long as it took Vance to leave. Then what? How would he get away?

She couldn't hang around, waiting for him at the entrance to the property.

Once away from the house, she craned around in hopes of spotting him through the thick growth. She was intent on the trees to the left when a sudden movement to the right made her whip around, jerking the wheel in the process.

"Simon!" she gasped.

Even as she swerved, he managed to hop directly over the passenger door and into the convertible.

"That was close," he said as she wrestled the car back under control. "I thought Laughlin wasn't supposed to be home."

"That was the idea. He wanted me to believe it so I wouldn't be on guard." Relieved that he'd made it out of the place without running into Vance, she glanced his way. He seemed more relaxed than she was feeling. "How close?"

"Another ten seconds and we would have been playing out a whole different scenario with the man."

An idea that made Phoebe a little woozy.

"Thank God that didn't happen. Wait a minute...what if he follows me?"

"By the time he changes the flat tire, we'll be long gone."

"Flat tire?" she echoed, suddenly smiling. "You found his car."

"Did I say that?"

He didn't have to. The startling grin splitting Simon's face was proof enough.

Leaving the property behind, Phoebe was starting to relax when he asked, "So, did you find anything?"

The second diary at the bottom of her bag made her shift in her seat. She gave him a noncommittal shrug. "Did you?"

"When you get back on the highway, find some place to pull over."

"Was that a yes?"

"Someplace discreet."

Five minutes later, Phoebe pulled into a large strip mall and parked amidst a sea of cars.

"So tell me," she demanded.

"Laughlin hid an envelope behind some books," he said, undoing the top button of his shirt.

"No wonder he was staring at that bookcase so intently!"

"I figured it would be in your best interests to leave everything the way I found it. Including the envelope, just in case he got suspicious enough to check for it. But I smuggled this out."

He pulled an eight-by-ten glossy from the confines of his shirt.

Audra in Boone's arms.

"She wasn't imagining it," Phoebe said softly, noting the unfamiliar setting.

Considering she could see the fan section of an airboat, the couple had to be embracing on a dock in the Glades. Behind them, a small weatherworn house stood on stilts that would take it above the rise of water even during the wettest of seasons. A love nest?

Something else Audra hadn't told her about.

"Vance *was* having Audra followed, then, just like she said. Spied on. Photographed. This is proof of his obsession with her."

"The police may not see a photograph of his wife and her lover as anything more significant than evidence for divorce proceedings."

"But he didn't want a divorce."

"Doesn't matter. He could say he knew the divorce was inevitable and he figured he needed some insurance so the judge would side with him when it came time to the financial settlement."

Phoebe didn't want to believe that their first real break was of no value. "But if we could get the investigator to talk, maybe he could give us something more substantial to use."

"No return address on the envelope."

Her spirits plummeted. "So we don't even know who took them."

"I didn't say that exactly. On the back of one of the photos, someone scrawled a number and a message to call Bubba at eight."

"So what are we waiting for? Let's find a phone and call this Bubba person."

"Don't get your hopes up too high. Bubba might not be talking. Or it could be nothing."

"And it could be something."

Besides, she had already been as low as she could get. Up was the only option left open to her.

THE PHONE NUMBER turned out to be that of the Osprey Nest, a bar on the road to Everglades City. Since he lived in the general vicinity, Simon knew the place. And being more or less acquainted with the bartender made it fairly easy to learn that Bubba was a regular.

On the walk back to her car, he related all that to Phoebe and promised, "I'll check it out tonight."

"You mean we, don't you?"

"If I meant we, I would have said so."

"What's the problem, Simon?"

She was the problem. Too headstrong...too daring...too tempting. She distracted him, and knowing the sort of clientele that frequented the Osprey Nest, he suspected he'd need all his faculties honed on his purpose.

What he told her was, "No need for both of us to cover the same tracks."

"I have nothing better to do with my evening."

When he said, "Try catching up on your reading," she started, and a becoming blush crept up her neck and into her cheeks.

For a moment, she seemed dumbfounded, and something more—guilty?—then she pulled her eyebrows together and glared at him.

"You have something against my company?"

"Not at all."

"Then, what?"

"The Osprey Nest is..."

"What? A bar? I'm half owner of a bar and grill, remember."

"I was going to say primitive."

Bikers and swampers together in the same bar could mean a volatile mix.

"You think I can't handle myself."

"No. I'm afraid you will. I don't want trouble."

Her mouth gaped open, but she snapped it shut just as quickly.

"Good, we're agreed, then," he said before she could regain her wits.

"Right," she said sweetly. "We'll each go on our own."

"Phoebe! You're being impossible."

"One of my best qualities."

Simon could tell he wasn't getting anywhere with this hardheaded woman. If he didn't take her with him, he feared she would make good on her threat. Having her under his thumb rated slightly above her showing up as a loose cannon.

Still, unused to caving, he narrowed his gaze at her. "Where will I find you?" He needed to get the upper hand in some way.

"When?"

"You have to eat."

"Then meet me at the Blue Crab." Turning a guileless smile on him, she added, "You are familiar with the place, aren't you?"

She was teasing him about showing up there unannounced that morning. Simon chose not to react, merely saying, "At eight."

Which would give Bubba plenty of time to get to Osprey Nest before them. Assuming the man would be there at all.

"Make it seven," she said.

"Why so early?"

"You have to eat, too."

The verbal byplay reminding him of his earlier go-around with Blair.

Then, again, he'd won that one…

HAVING SEVERAL HOURS to kill, Simon decided to spend them at Calderon Charters, ostensibly to learn more about the business, but in reality to get better acquainted with Elise Navarro. He suspected she still had much stronger feelings for Boone than his ex-fiancée had ever had.

Elijah Greer, the wizened black man who'd given Elise water when she had her fainting spell, was in her office when Simon tapped at the door. Seeing Simon, Elijah frowned and slid off the desk, where he'd been sitting. He said something to Elise in a low tone, then made for the exit, barely nodding at Simon as he went.

"You have messages."

Wondering how anyone could know he would be there, he asked, "Who from?"

"A vendor. Boone's lawyer. And Blair Ratcliff."

He didn't miss the slight shift in Elise's expression at the mention of the other woman. She picked at the half-eaten lunch at her elbow.

"Blair called?" he mused aloud, just to get her reaction.

"She wanted you to know something came up and she couldn't meet you at seven for dinner tomorrow night, after all." Elise couldn't quite mask her disapproval. "She said to make it at nine instead."

The time Blair had wanted to meet in the first place. So he hadn't actually won anything at all in that corner, Simon thought wryly. Though Elise's curiosity certainly seemed piqued. Now that could be promising. Choosing to make the most of the opportunity, he parked himself on the edge of the desk in front of hers.

"Tell me about my brother's ex-fiancée."

"She's rich and, unless you're blind, you know she's model-beautiful," Elise said as if she'd compared herself and felt she'd come up lacking.

"I wasn't asking about the obvious."

"What, then?"

"I was wondering what went wrong between her and Boone? Before Audra," he qualified.

Elise toyed with a sandwich half, showing a greater interest in the food than Simon figured she really had. Because she didn't relish thinking about Boone's relationship with another woman?

Then, as if making up her mind to satisfy his curiosity, she set down the food and said, "Your brother wasn't ambitious enough to satisfy Blair's daddy. And she couldn't make him toe the line."

"What line?"

"Name it. Everything had to be her way. She wasn't interested in what Boone wanted, whether it had to do with business...or their wedding plans." Her expression hardening her pretty features, she added, "Blair Ratcliff is what we common folk call a royal bitch."

Not having expected her to be so direct, Simon arched his eyebrows. "But tell me how you *really* feel."

Elise's bronzed face grew ruddy. "Sorry. I assumed you wanted honesty."

"Honesty *is* what I want."

But how much would she give him?

If he asked her directly about her own relationship to Boone, would she deny there had been anything personal between them?

He said, "Even so, Boone obviously loved Blair. I found the engagement ring last night. The inscription said it all. *Forever...*"

She smirked. "That doesn't tell you a thing about the way it really was."

"What makes you say that?"

"Boone had nothing to do with that ring but pay for it. Blair's daddy is this big-deal, world-famous jeweler. She had the ring custom-designed for herself and had the bill sent to your brother. You have to appreciate the irony—when the bill arrived, Boone was trying to figure out how to break it off with her nice and clean."

"Was that before or after he met Audra?"

"Before...I—I guess."

Elise appeared uncertain. Did that mean she wasn't as privy to his brother's life as he'd suspected...or that Boone had been trying to keep his affair with Audra quiet since both Blair and Laughlin continued to be part of the picture? Blair had indicated Audra had come between her and Boone, but that could have been part of her face-saving routine.

"My brother must've been pretty ticked to tell you about the ring."

"Boone told me lots of things," she murmured, sounding a little lost. "We were...close."

How close?

Simon didn't want to put her on guard by asking.

He figured if he played it smart, she'd eventually tell him what he wanted to know…one way or the other.

"Odd," he said instead.

"What?"

"About the inscription, I mean. Why would Blair have the sentiment *Forever* engraved in the ring if she was dissatisfied enough with the relationship to end it?"

"Blair told you *she* broke the engagement?" Elise sounded strangled. "Oh, add liar to bitch! You should have heard her when he told her it was over—she was fit to be tied! She said no man humiliated her and got away with it. She also said he'd be sorry."

"My brother told you all this?"

"I heard it with my own ears."

An interesting turn of events. "Then he broke the news to her here at the office."

"No, at the house." Her hazel eyes widened slightly. "Um, I'd stopped by to drop off some work," she said unconvincingly. "Blair didn't know I was in the other room. She goaded Boone…and he must've gotten angry enough to forget about me when he finally gave her the boot."

Simon thought about the open layout of the first floor of his brother's home. What other room? The bathroom? Or had she been waiting for him in a room upstairs like the master bedroom?

With his suspicions about Boone and his attractive assistant pretty much confirmed, he asked, "Did she ever carry through with her threat?"

"Threat?" she echoed.

"To make him sorry?"

Suddenly seeming uncomfortable, she shrugged. "I—I have no idea."

"Boone never mentioned anything?"

Elise's thick dark eyebrows furrowed. "Why is it you're suddenly sounding like a cop?"

"My apologies. I got caught up in your story, I guess. You can't blame me for being curious."

But she wasn't so easily appeased. "A little late to get interested in your brother, isn't it?"

The criticism being his invitation to leave it be for the moment.

Only Simon couldn't.

Even though he knew Boone might have done it—knew his brother had been capable of watching a person whom he loved die—Simon wished with all his soul to prove that this time, Boone had been the victim.

"I loved my brother more than anyone in the world."

Elise appeared disbelieving. "That's why you never showed your face around here."

"We had our differences."

"You didn't even come to his funeral, but you're quick enough to grab onto his estate."

Coldly angry, he informed her, "His house...this business...they mean nothing to me."

"Then why are you here? Why aren't you hiding in your swamp as usual?"

"Because I want to find the murderer." The words were out of his mouth too quickly.

"Murderer?" Elise went wide-eyed.

Not exactly subtle, Calderon.

Then, again, perhaps this situation didn't call for subtlety. Perhaps the shock value would give him an edge.

"Murderer. As in the person who killed Boone. And Audra. Or do you, his good friend, really believe he did it?"

"But the authorities—"

"Adopted an easy theory."

Was Elise nervous or just shocked at his revelation? Her face had paled, and her arms were crossed around her middle as if she was holding herself together. Simon hadn't forgotten her first reaction to him.

"No telling how hard the police are working on finding other suspects." He slid away from the desk. "I'd better get to those messages."

And figure out a way to get to the woman who might know more about his brother's death than she was letting on.

"YOU MIGHT AS WELL eat without him, Pheebs," Kevin suggested as he poured beers for what looked to be an entire football team, "or the food'll get cold."

Almost eight and no Simon.

Kevin had done his best to mellow her mood, but Phoebe's patience was worn thin. Defiantly, she grabbed a giant shrimp from the seafood platter she'd had prepared specially for them and stuck it into her mouth whole.

"Great," she muttered over her mouthful, "it's just about cold already."

And she'd lost her appetite waiting. The shrimp went down hard and settled like a rock in her stomach. She'd given Simon the benefit of the doubt when he hadn't appeared at seven, had even waited an extra half hour before telling the cook to start her order. He'd made them a huge platter of his specialties— garlic shrimp, deep-fried conch fritters with cilantro-lime sauce and pan-fried oysters, all arranged beautifully on a bed of rice pilaf and garnished with fresh chunks of pineapple and mango.

To think she'd wanted to impress Simon Calderon. And why? Because she couldn't stop thinking about the man, couldn't stop feeling his bedroom gaze on her...

Crazed hormones were responsible.

Lust, pure and simple.

Now Simon was so late that Phoebe suspected he was on his way to Osprey Nest without her. Which probably had been his plan all along. Disappointed and angry, she was trying to decide on her next move.

Kevin said, "Maybe Calderon's not showing is for the best. I mean, it sounds like he's trying to protect you, Pheebs. Why fight it?"

She glared at her partner. "I don't need protection from anyone."

"How about from yourself?"

Practically the same thing Simon had implied.

If he was so concerned, why had he left her to her own devices after she'd threatened to go alone?

"Do you realize how annoying you can be?" she snapped.

"Hey, I'm on your side," Kevin reminded her.

"The Osprey Nest isn't anything like the Blue Crab. I know that place. It's pretty rough."

Again, like Simon!

"So what's the worst that can happen to me there?"

"Use your imagination. Look what happened to Audra."

Phoebe didn't want to. But a flash of her sister floating facedown in the pool, her lifeblood seeping into the water, came to her anyway.

Swallowing hard, she said, "Audra wasn't at that bar when she died."

"But would you ever have believed anyone would murder her? And she was someplace you undoubtedly considered safe."

She wasn't about to admit he had a valid point, of course, but Phoebe was getting more upset by the moment. She bit into a conch fritter as she slid off the bar stool. Her mind was made up. She was going to the Osprey Nest—alone.

"I don't know why I tell you anything."

"Because you know I care about you...even if you sometimes don't have any more sense than one of those shellfish you like so much."

"Thanks loads."

Kevin reached over the bar and gently clasped onto her wrist. "Give it up, Pheebs, please."

His expression was beseeching, as if he really did fear something bad might happen to her. She pulled her arm away.

"I can't give it up."

"Why not?" he persisted, suddenly sounding angry. "Why won't you leave the investigation to the professionals, when that's what they're paid to do?"

"Because finding the truth about Audra's murder isn't a job to me like it is to them, Kevin. It's personal." *Why couldn't he understand?* "I lost one of the best parts of my life. I won't rest until I know why."

Kevin didn't say anything more, merely stared at her, his expression now reflecting her own anger and frustration back at her.

A weird feeling suddenly gripped Phoebe, an impression that Kevin's reaction was *too* strong. He cared about her, of course, but could more be involved here? Surely not. Surely he was only being a good friend.

Sighing, Phoebe turned away from him only to walk straight into a man drawing up behind her.

Hands gripping her upper arms to steady her, he asked, "Going somewhere without me?"

Chapter Seven

Gaping at Simon, Phoebe wasn't certain how to react to his arrival.

He was looking more tempting than she'd ever seen him—tight, worn jeans and a thin T-shirt emphasizing a body that had been honed to near perfection, undoubtedly by physical labor. (She couldn't visualize him working out in a gym...) A sweep of dark hair grazed his forehead and dramatized the dark intensity of his deepset, hooded eyes.

Heart pounding, washed by a sense of relief that he hadn't made a fool of her, after all, Phoebe chose anger to mask her reaction.

"You!" she said accusingly. "I thought—"

"I can only imagine," he said dryly. "What? It's strictly a woman's prerogative to be late?"

She nearly bit her tongue after saying, "You could have called—dinner's cold." The second time that day she'd sounded pathetically like a wife.

He glanced at the platter. "But it still looks pretty good to me. How about throwing it in a container. We can eat while we drive."

Phoebe realized this was a defining moment in their working relationship. She could choose to verbally string him up by his ears about being late, or she could choose to be as cooperative as she wished him to be. Somehow, she couldn't see that lecturing him would get her what she wanted.

So she got hold of herself and said, "Sure. Give me a couple of minutes." Remembering Kevin, she turned back to the bar, saying, "By the way, this is my partner…"

Her introduction trailed off as she realized Kevin had moved away from them without saying a word. Elbows wedged on the edge of the bar some ways down, he was leaning into a pretty customer's space and saying something that was making her laugh. This one was a brunette. Expanding his horizons? she mused, knowing his current penchant for blondes.

"He seems to be otherwise occupied."

"Give him a minute." Her partner's concern for her had certainly dwindled fast in the light of an attractive woman's arrival. "As soon as he gets her vital statistics and a phone number, he'll be back."

Phoebe went for that container and her shoulder bag. But when she returned to the bar a few minutes later, Kevin was still preoccupied. And Simon was wolfing down a conch fritter. She checked the platter. He'd been doing a creditable job of decimating the seafood while waiting for her.

"These are great," he said.

"When they're hot, they're fantastic." Her appetite returning with a vengeance, she popped an oyster into her mouth and unceremoniously slid the remaining food into the container. ''Ready when you are.''

''Then let's get going.''

Phoebe noticed Kevin didn't even look up as they walked by...as if he were studiously ignoring her. So unlike him. What was his problem? First being over-protective. Now acting like...what?

Again, the weird feeling...

Surely Kevin couldn't dislike Simon sight unseen.

Before going out the door, she glanced back over her shoulder and caught her partner staring after them. Unsmiling. Seemingly focused on Simon.

Uneasy, Phoebe led the way out.

THE OSPREY NEST sort of looked like one. While not perched in the branches of a tree, the unpainted, weathered wood structure had been built on stilts for protection against flooding, as had many buildings in this neck of the Glades.

A passenger this time, Phoebe noted the motorcy-cles lined up between old beaters and all sorts of util-ity vehicles. Simon himself was driving a well-aged pickup. Undoubtedly, he'd fit right in with the bar's crowd.

He whipped into an open space and killed the en-gine, but made no move to get out. ''I'm setting some ground rules before we go in.''

''Like what?''

''Like I do all the talking. Like, you stick to me like glue. Like, you follow my lead no matter what. Agreed?''

While she yearned to make a crack—call him Your

Macho-ness, perhaps—his tone stopped her. This was a different Simon from the one she'd been experiencing all day. This was the closed, angry man who'd kicked her out of his brother's house, a man who wouldn't stand for any argument from her...or anyone else, she was certain.

And probably that was for the best.

"Agreed."

The night was still and humid and crowded with swamp noises. They'd arrived at the edge of civilization. Phoebe felt as if they were crossing the line into the wild.

Upon entering the establishment teeming with rowdy men, she was certain of it. A raw energy electrified the smoke-filled place and immediately put her on edge.

There were only three other women that she could see. One was a harried waitress slapping away roving hands as she tried to deliver a drink order. The other two were partnered with raunchy, bearded guys wearing leather vests over otherwise bare torsos. When yet another of the bikers leered at *her,* Phoebe was thankful she hadn't come alone. She squeezed closer to Simon.

He gave her a quick, assessing look. "Problem?"

She shook her head. "What now?"

"Like I said...follow my lead."

He started through the horde, Phoebe close behind. The few tables were crowded, as was the neon-lit bar. More rough-looking men filled the standing room and shouted at each other over the wail from the jukebox—a woman complaining about her carousing man.

A few gave her such a thorough once-over that she gladly became Simon's shadow. Although he was acting as if she wasn't there, she was pretty sure he sensed her every twitch. When a middle-aged Cuban caught her attention, showing off his gold front teeth and silently indicating he'd buy her a drink, Simon gave him a chilling frown.

"The lady's with me."

That's all it took to persuade the man to go back to his compadres.

Simon and Kevin had both been correct about this not being her kind of place. The Osprey Nest. How fitting, the osprey being a predator. The bar was filled with them.

Simon elbowed their way up to the bar and ordered two draft beers without first consulting her. Though Phoebe wasn't particularly fond of the stuff, she didn't dare protest. She merely lifted the mug and took an obligatory if small sip.

"Keep the change," Simon said, giving the bartender a ten. "Seen Bubba tonight?"

"Over there." The man indicated the pool table in the back corner.

Whipping his free hand around Phoebe's waist and snuggling her closer to his side than made her comfortable, Simon led her toward the knot of men hunkered around the green felt-covered table. She grew warm and blamed it on the beer, even though she'd barely taken a sip.

Or maybe she was experiencing the adrenaline rush of doing something slightly dangerous.

Anything to negate the possibility that Simon had that potent an effect on her...

Ahead, a few more women mixed with the crowd around the pool table. Each clung to her companion. One slid a bold hand down her boyfriend's stomach and trailed it across an upper thigh. He gave her a hot, suggestive look.

Phoebe turned away...her gaze meeting Simon's.

Did he notice her discomfort?

He dipped his head so his lips were at her ear. "You could take a few tips..." he whispered.

Though his warm breath made Phoebe catch her breath, she muttered, "Keep dreaming."

Deliberately ignoring him, she focused her attention at the far end of the pool table. There a stocky man wearing a wrinkled tropical-print shirt and a baseball cap let out a whoop and victoriously waved his cue stick in the air.

The short man next to him slapped a bill into his free hand. "Guess tonight's your night, Bubba."

The man they'd come to find...

Bubba slid the money into an already bulging shirt pocket. "Who's next?" A grin splitting his jowly face, he turned a beady gaze on the man closest to him.

"Not me."

The next one threw up his hands. "I'm dry."

But a skinny guy on his other side said, "I got a ten to kill."

"Well, step right up, son," Bubba said, whomping the cue stick on the floor. "I'm a thirsty man."

As the competitors stepped up to the table, Phoebe

wondered what Simon was waiting for. She nudged him with her shoulder, which he ignored.

"Aren't you going to talk to him?" she whispered. His only answer was a hard waist-squeeze… prompting a squeak from her.

Good grief…she wasn't even supposed to talk to him now?

Simon's gaze was fixed on the table action. For the next several minutes, he didn't take his eyes from Bubba. Phoebe could almost hear the wheels turning as he studied the man's every efficient move until he blew what looked to be a pretty easy bank shot.

Grinning, his opponent started taking down balls but missed the fourth.

On his next turn, Bubba won the game.

Pocketing the money practically before the eight rolled into its pocket, he asked, "Rematch?"

"On an IOU?"

Bubba snorted. "Yeah, right." His gaze swept the room for a likely candidate. "Cash only. How about you, son?"

The chosen one said, "I'm through for the night."

"And I'm no fool," his companion added.

"No guts, no glory!" Bubba stated, again whacking the end of his cue stick to the floor.

Then Simon let go of Phoebe's waist and stepped forward. "I've got a few guts. Some cash, too. A C-note."

Which he plunked down on the edge of the table to the appreciative murmur of the audience.

"Whoa, big spender," someone behind Phoebe muttered.

"Who is this guy?" another whispered.

"Don't know, but I seen him here before. Usually keeps to himself."

A not unexpected impression, Phoebe thought, wondering if anyone really knew Simon Calderon.

"You break," Bubba said.

"Don't mind if I do."

Simon racked the balls, then shot the cue ball into their midst, sending them rolling in every direction. Two stripes and one solid whipped into pockets.

He called, "Stripes," then took a moment to study the layout before methodically cleaning them off the table.

Bubba's smile faded as their numbers diminished to one. Unfortunately, Simon's thirteen ball stopped just short of a corner pocket.

"Lucky thirteen," Bubba said, his grin returning. "Well, now, ain't this interesting."

The grin lasted all the way to his last ball. His six was lined up with the thirteen for the same pocket. If he kicked in Simon's ball—which was inevitable, Phoebe thought—he would lose. The only option left to him was another bank shot.

Which he missed, exactly as he had in the last game.

Had Simon somehow planned it that way?

Phoebe's own skills at pool were amateurish at best. But she knew a shark could leave a ball anywhere on the table at will. She watched Simon quickly take out his remaining ball followed by the eight.

Several people cheered.

One of them said, "Hey, whaddya know, Bubba? You ain't infallible tonight, after all."

Grudgingly, the stocky man emptied his shirt pocket and turned virtually all of his night's winnings over to Simon. Left with a ten-dollar bill, he held it up. "Rematch?"

"You said you were thirsty. How about I buy you a drink instead."

"Yeah, why not," Bubba grumbled.

Finally. Phoebe took a deep, satisfied breath.

A handful of men were leaving a table, which Bubba skillfully commandeered before anyone else could get near it. Simon immediately sat, but Bubba pulled out a chair for her.

"Here you go, little lady."

"The name's Phoebe. He's Simon."

Signaling a waitress, Bubba whipped a second chair around so its back was facing the table. "Where'd you learn to play like that, son?" he asked as he straddled the seat.

"Here and there." Simon placed the hundred and Bubba's tens and twenties between them. "How'd you like another chance at this?"

"Two hundred? You gotta be kiddin'. I'm busted."

"I don't mean gambling. I'm talking about a sure thing. A trade."

Bubba's thick eyebrows pulled together and his eyes narrowed. "What kinda trade?"

"Information."

"About...?"

Phoebe jumped in. "Vance Laughlin." And ignored Simon's immediate glower.

Bubba hesitated a moment too long to be believable before saying, ''Don't recollect the name.''

''Maybe your memory just needs a jog.''

Simon slid another hundred onto the pile as the harried waitress drew up to their table.

''What can I get you folks?''

''Beers all around,'' Simon told her.

''None for me,'' Phoebe quickly said, then turned to Bubba. ''Vance Laughlin is a successful Fort Myers businessman. You sent him some photographs. Don't bother to deny it. You left your calling card on one of them.''

''Could be, I suppose…''

Simon pulled out yet another hundred and waggled it in front of the man's face.

Bubba licked his lips, hesitated a moment, then took the bill and started to scoop up the money from the table until Simon slapped a hand onto the pile.

''Information first.''

''Okay, so I *do* remember a Laughlin.''

''He hired you to follow my sister Audra, right?''

''Phoebe!''

Ignoring Simon's growl, she demanded, ''Well, didn't he?''

''Not exactly. I have this contact…a lawyer in Naples.''

Simon's gaze was steely when he said, ''I assume you remember *his* name.''

''Yeah, sure. Only I ain't gonna ruin a good thing. Know what I mean? I do jobs for him every once in a while.''

''And you can keep on doing them. We're not going to squeal on you. It wouldn't be to our advantage.'' When Bubba squinted at them as if trying to make up his mind, Simon added, ''Or you can forget about the four hundred. *A lawyer in Naples* isn't enough information to be worth this kind of money.''

''Yeah, okay!'' Bubba immediately snapped. ''I believe you won't say nothing. Name's Don Platt.''

''If an intermediary hired you,'' Phoebe mused, ''why did you contact Vance yourself?''

''Figured he might like some extra copies of the wife,'' Bubba said as the beers arrived.

And obviously he'd wanted some extra money, she thought, figuring the extra photos had been a basis of blackmail. What had he done? Threatened to sell them to the Florida Investigator?

She wondered how much more it would cost to get him to divulge details of his meeting with her brother-in-law. Before she could try to get anything out of him, however, he snatched the money, grabbed a fresh mug and stood.

''Thanks for the beer, son.''

''Wait a minute,'' Phoebe protested. ''I was just getting started. I have more questions.''

''But I ain't got no more answers.'' With a grin, Bubba shoved the money into his pantspocket. ''Be seeing you, little lady.''

''Aren't you going to stop him?'' Phoebe asked Simon as the man strolled back through the crowd.

He paid the waitress, then said, ''Old Bubba's told us all he's going to.''

''You don't know that.''

"He didn't suggest I come up with another offer, did he?"

"No." She glanced back the way Bubba had gone, but he'd already disappeared from sight. "At least we got something out of him. A lawyer in Naples...how strange."

"Not when your sister was living there."

"Maybe not the Naples part, but why a lawyer instead of a private investigation service?"

"Platt might have been someone Vance already knew. Someone he'd worked with on a deal."

Which would make a certain amount of sense.

"Now the question is, how do we get a lawyer to breach his confidentiality agreement?"

"Without his knowing it."

"You mean...do something illegal like breaking into his office?"

"That's one option."

One that Phoebe didn't care for. She'd had enough of a scare with Vance himself.

"What are the others?" she asked.

"That'll take some thought. In the meantime, let's get out of here."

He got no argument from her. Phoebe was willing and ready to ditch the place. Simon shouldered his way through the crowd and again pulled her with him. She convinced herself that her relief at getting outside was due to the smoky, claustrophobic feel of the bar rather than his letting go of her.

She kept some distance between them as they made their way back to the truck.

Upon arriving at the vehicle, however, she immediately noticed something out of whack. The truck was listing deeply toward the driver's side.

"You didn't park on soft ground, did you?" she asked, unable to remember anything unusual.

"Crushed shell and gravel."

They drew closer.

Even in the dim light of the parking lot, she could see that the problem lay with both driver's-side tires. Simon swiftly approached the truck and stooped down near the rear wheel to check it.

"Two flats?" she asked.

"Two slashed tires." His tone was grim.

She trembled inside as she asked, "But...how... who...?" *And why?* "What reason would anyone have to play such a nasty trick on you?"

Or had the trick been on both of them?

Bubba?

"Maybe whoever it was just didn't like my looks."

Simon straightened and slowly inspected his surroundings as if he expected to zero in on the guilty party.

Phoebe followed suit.

The skin along her spine crawled. She felt as if the night had a thousand eyes, all aimed their way. Anyone could be watching them from the dark.

"I'm going to need new tires," he said, breaking her concentration. "And that's not going to happen before morning."

"But we're in the middle of nowhere!" she croaked. "What do you suggest we do?"

"Start walking."

"Back to Marco?"

Was he crazy?

Opening the driver's door, he said, "To my place," then reached inside.

"You live around here?"

He pulled out and tested a flashlight. It worked, for which she was thankful. "More or less."

"Which is it?" she persisted. "More? Or less?"

"That would probably be more."

"How *much* more?"

Simon slammed the truck door and strolled toward her. "If you want, you can go back inside and call a taxi. I'm sure one will come...eventually."

Inside. Where the perpetrator of the nasty prank might be expecting them.

"You'll wait with me, right?"

"I'm walking."

He was. Straight past her. Phoebe was appalled. And caught between a rock and a hard place...or rather, between Simon and the men inside the Osprey Nest. Including whoever held the grudge.

She only took a second to wonder which option would prove the more dangerous—

"Wait up!"

Phoebe scrambled after him as she was certain Simon knew she would. He didn't even shorten his stride to accommodate her. Her imagination heightened, she felt as if someone were watching them now.

"Bubba?" she said aloud.

"What about him?"

She peered over her shoulder between vehicles and into the dark beyond. Her gaze swept in every direction but she didn't see so much as a hint of movement. And yet, the sensation of being watched lingered.

"He did disappear pretty quickly after leaving the table," she reminded Simon. "Do you think he's the one who took a knife to your tires?"

"Why would he?"

"You tricked him into giving you information."

"I paid him. And well, at that."

Simon stopped dead in his tracks and focused on a stand of trees to their left...

Pulse immediately surging, she stopped, too, and whispered, "What?"

"Shh." He tilted his head slightly, as if listening to some sound she couldn't hear. After a moment, he muttered, "Nothing," and moved on.

"Don't scare me like that!"

Realizing that Simon was every bit as wary of their surroundings as she was didn't reassure Phoebe in the least. But it did keep her close to his side.

Their arms brushed, the contact shooting a further thrill through her, albeit one of a very different sort. On edge again, she attempted to conquer both fear and attraction with logic. She resumed her train of thought.

"You set Bubba up with the pool game to get to him," she said. "He doesn't seem like the type who would tolerate being played with."

"Probably not...if there was nothing in it for him. He came away with his pocket three hundred heavier."

After leaving the bar's parking lot they were walking in the dark, and Phoebe wondered why Simon didn't switch on the flashlight.

"Who else, then?" she asked.

"Your guess is as good as mine."

Vance was the only other name that came readily to mind. Had her brother-in-law somehow figured out the purpose of her visit? And that Simon had been with her?

"Could Vance have been following us all day?" she wondered aloud.

"Unlikely...but possible."

"Then you didn't notice anyone keeping up with us on the way here."

"Not a soul."

But he was looking behind them now as if he expected someone to pop out at them. A thought that made breathing normally difficult.

The area around them was suddenly bathed in a pale light as a vehicle swept down on them. Simon pulled her off the road. A moment later, a truck raced by.

"We'd better stick to the shoulder."

"What there is of it," she muttered, unhappy with the uneven, sometimes squishy footing. Walking along the side of a narrow road like this could be treacherous in full daylight. "How in the heck can you see where you're going?"

"Experience."

Living in the swamp equipped him with night eyes? Night hearing, too, she guessed. She, however, having lived her whole life in more civilized surroundings, was not so blessed.

"If you're not going to use your flashlight, I'll gladly take it."

"Here."

Simon placed it in her hand. The brush of his fingers against her palm distracted her for a moment…made her catch her breath…

"Are you going to carry it around like a makeshift weapon or use it so you can see where you're going?"

"Oh."

That he sounded amused brought warmth to Phoebe's cheeks. At least he couldn't see *that* in the dark.

She snapped on the flashlight and stared down at the ground, keeping one eye open for ankle-twisting stones or mud holes, the other for anything that slithered. She couldn't help wondering what she was doing hiking in the middle of nowhere, practically in the middle of the night. She had to be out of her mind.

"Why are you making me come to your place with you?" she asked, her displeasure with the situation growing with each step she took.

A car swept past them, moving in the opposite direction, while another set of lights shimmered in the distance.

"I didn't make you do anything."

"You left me with no choice."

"If you didn't have taxi fare, you could have said so."

Something about his tone got to her.

Vaguely aware of another vehicle behind them traveling in their direction, she refused to be distracted from this debate. "You were counting on my not wanting to go back inside alone. Why?"

"Why should I have thought you would object?" he countered smoothly. "You were set on storming the Osprey Nest alone in search of Bubba if I didn't take you."

"That's before I knew what the place was like..." Her sentence faded as his intent crystallized. "Wait a minute. Is that what's going on here? You forced me to walk to who-knows-where in the dark because you needed to hear me say you were right?"

"That'd be a pleasant change," he muttered as the vehicle behind them roared closer.

"Hey, how fast is that guy going?"

Phoebe glanced over her shoulder only to be blinded by high beams. Shading her eyes, she blinked and squinted against the bright light...

Just as it swerved directly toward them!

Chapter Eight

Using a full body tackle, Simon flung Phoebe out of the path of the speeding vehicle with mere seconds to spare. He rolled them both over a slight embankment even as a dark four-wheel-drive truck careened by them with a roar and a spew of mud and decaying plant matter.

They landed several yards from the road, limbs tangled, him on top. The moon had come out from behind the clouds and its light revealed Phoebe's face, frightened and muck-splashed. She lay still beneath him, trembling, and for once, speechless.

"Are you all right?" he asked.

He drew his gaze away from her, automatically seeking out the bastard who'd almost run them down.

"I—I g-guess," she said. "What the devil was that person th-thinking?"

Simon connected with the road. Red lights glowed in the distance.

Brake lights.

"Nothing good for us."

As much as he would have liked to remain exactly

as they were for a while—the feel of her body under his again something he'd been imagining since their first encounter—Simon knew better than to waste precious seconds. Untangling himself gingerly so that he wouldn't hurt her further, he shot to his feet and helped Phoebe to hers.

"Can you stand on your own?" Even as he asked, the vehicle made a U-turn, tires squealing.

"Yeah. I'm just a little shaky."

"Good." Not trusting the driver's intentions, he grabbed her hand. "Then let's get going."

He'd had a feeling those slashed tires had merely been a diversion. A means to a bad end...for them.

That's why he'd been determined to keep Phoebe at his side. Thank God, he'd been able to trick her into coming with him.

"Wait a minute." She stood fast. "Where's the flashlight?"

"It must have gone out when you tossed it." He started pulling the stubborn woman away from the road whether she wanted to go or not. "I don't need it and neither do you...unless you want to be a moving target."

"What?"

"The vehicle's heading back our way."

"The driver probably wants to make sure we weren't hurt."

"That's one possibility," he said tersely.

She stopped resisting. "I don't think I want to hear the other one."

Sure enough, the four-wheel-drive slammed to a

stop near the spot where they'd taken their nose dive. A moment later, a brilliant beam flashed along the ground.

If only the driver really was trying to make certain they'd come out of their nosedive intact...

Not believing that for a moment, Simon headed straight for a nearby cypress stand that would give them cover. Behind them, the searchlight began skimming an increasingly wide area...advancing fast... nearly catching up to them.

"Hurry!"

For once, Phoebe didn't challenge him.

They ran, quickly reaching the initial scattering of dwarf cypress trees sprouting out of small pockets of water. No matter that they moved as swiftly as the uneven terrain would allow, the beam of light intercepted them.

Her turning to look back slowed them a bit. Glancing behind them as well, Simon realized the driver had spotted them and the vehicle's powerful engine revved to life.

"Come on!"

Simon tugged at Phoebe to make her move faster. Instead, she slipped on the muck underfoot and went down to her knees with a splash. She almost brought him with her. He resisted the fall, caught her around the waist and dragged her straight toward the heart of the cypress dome.

"He's gaining on us," she croaked.

The roar of the engine closing the distance behind

them made him move faster than he would normally with someone unfamiliar with thc territory in tow.

They were crashing through thigh-high saw grass immersed in inches—sometimes a couple of feet—of water. And as the distance between the cypress trunks narrowed, they had to fight hanging Spanish moss that whipped them in the face and chest. Phoebe was having trouble keeping her footing over the knotted roots. She didn't complain, but Simon found himself half-carrying her.

What choice did he have?

The all-terrain four-by-four would soon be upon them, unless they made it to the denser center of the dome, where the water was deeper, allowing the cypress trees to grow not only taller but closer together.

Too close for any vehicle to squeeze through.

With the instinct of a swamper guiding him, he flew along, knowing that once their pursuer couldn't go any further except on foot, they would be safe. This was his territory. His home. He could travel through it blindfolded.

Not so whoever sat behind the wheel.

It didn't take a genius to guess the driver's intentions. The bastard would run them down and leave their carcasses to rot in the swamp.

And Simon didn't fancy being alligator bait.

PHOEBE THOUGHT her lungs might explode before Simon slowed. Of course, he really had no choice. While they'd raced through arduous territory for what had seemed like hours, but had really been only minutes, the terrain had become nearly impossible to negotiate.

Ears attuned to the slightest sound, she could hardly hear the engine anymore.

"I think we're losing him," she gasped as she sank to mid-thigh in the murky water.

"That's the idea."

A hiss to their left made her jump but didn't even slow him. "Alligators?"

"This is their natural habitat," he agreed.

Because he didn't sound too worried, she asked, "Neighbors of yours?"

"Could be, though I don't know them all by sight."

She shuddered in response. He pulled her closer. Her heart lurched...as if it hadn't had a good enough aerobic workout already.

"Do you know where we are?"

"A general idea."

"You mean we're lost?"

"I mean the swamp doesn't exactly have road signs." He pointed overhead to a blissfully clear sky. "But we do have the stars to map our direction."

"So you can get us out of here, right? *Soon?*" she emphasized.

"Soon enough."

A moment later, they'd risen to higher ground. Wet, mucky peat lay beneath their feet, but at least they weren't wading anymore.

"When I get home, I'm going to throw away these sneakers," she vowed, feet squishing in them.

"Or you could use them as decoration with those swamp creatures that inhabit your house," Simon suggested in a serious tone. "They'll serve as a reminder."

"Of what?" she asked. "This is one night that I'm not likely to forget."

No doubt he meant as a reminder of her hardheadedness at insisting on going to the Osprey Nest.

But all he said was, "Stop a minute and catch your breath."

Glad to do as he ordered, Phoebe propped her back against a cypress tree.

He let go but didn't move away.

Even so, she regretted the break of contact. For some odd reason, Simon's hanging on to her had been more than physically necessary. It had been comforting, as well.

"You all right?" he asked, close enough that his breath warmed her already overheated face.

"Uh-huh," she lied.

She might be intact physically, but she'd never been so frightened. Then again, she'd never had anyone try to run her over before.

He ran the back of his knuckles along her cheek, making her catch her breath.

"You're trembling."

"Not used to the exercise."

"Liar."

He was crowding her, still touching her with one hand, while his other flattened the tree trunk beside her face. Though his body was inches from hers, she imagined them clinging together...naked.

Vaguely remembering the reason they'd been forced to run, she whispered, "Don't you have anything more productive to do than hassle a woman who's too exhausted to defend herself properly?"

"Well, then..."

His head dipped slow enough that it gave her time to duck if that's what she wanted to do.

She didn't.

Willingly, she raised her face to his. Her heart hadn't yet settled, and when their lips touched, it pumped double time. Gladly, she parted her lips and invited him in.

For a moment, she floated, her mind wandering to places drawn by passion, painted by ecstasy.

For a moment, she knew exactly what it would be like to be taken by this man and to take in return.

For a moment, she was unresisting.

Until the kiss ended. Too brief, she thought, too tender. That he didn't move away made her self-conscious.

"Simon..."

She tried to make her hands do what she bade them, to push him away, but they wouldn't cooperate.

"Phoebe," he murmured in return, rubbing his face in her hair.

His lips trailed a path down the side of her neck, found the sweet spot at the juncture of her shoulder. His tasting her was the most erotic sensation...

And then he pulled away.

Now she felt truly naked.

Vulnerable...

And remembered the reason they were on the run.

What if they were playing into the villain's hands by stopping at all?

"Do you think he's close behind us?" she asked, not understanding how she could be so torn between two different instincts.

Survival...and sex.

That the person who'd tried running them over was still after them wasn't even a question in her mind.

"I'll find out."

"Wait!" Her cry as he moved away fell on deaf ears. "Simon," she hissed, "don't leave me here alone."

"Stay put!"

Within seconds he became one with his swamp.

Leaving Phoebe to the dark and the dangerous creatures who roamed it...

She'd barely taken a few easy breaths and now her chest was tightening up again. Every sound seemed laced with menace.

A scrabbling like that of a raccoon made the skin along her spine crawl.

A splash pressed her hard into the tree trunk.

A slither would send her right up the damn tree!

Not normally a cowardly person, Phoebe felt completely out of her element. She loved watching the creatures of southwestern Florida...even at night, as long as it was from the safety of her own screened-in lanai. Her years of exploring the Glades had been confined to group activities and daylight hours, when she'd been able to recognize the dangers around her.

All that had changed in a heartbeat, she realized.

Alligators…

Poisonous snakes…

Someone who'd tried to kill them…

All were out there waiting.

Phoebe hugged herself, wishing she could urge her mind to a kinder, gentler, safer path…

UNENCUMBERED BY PHOEBE, Simon became one with the Glades, a ghost.

Silent, invisible, invincible, he circled back.

Aware of every croak, every footfall, every hiss…

His hearing was as sharp as that of any swamp creature.

He was one of them, always had been.

As his twin had been, until Boone had chosen a different path…

Growing up in backwater country, he and Boone had been able to lose themselves in their wilderness so completely that even their father, himself a lifelong swamper, had been unable to track them if they hadn't wanted to be found. Their father had taught them well.

Perhaps too well.

A memory of the last time they'd all been out here together crystallized…

Realizing what was happening, Simon tore his mind away from the memories and aimed his thoughts back where they belonged.

He'd been wrong and Phoebe had been right all along. He knew it now. If Boone had been guilty, no one would have followed them.

No one would have tried to kill them.

For surely that was the reality of the situation. No one would try running over two people with a four-by-four vehicle as a prank. The slashed tires hadn't been a prank, either, he decided, not even a nasty one.

Someone had wanted them on foot.

Vulnerable.

Dead.

Because they were asking too many questions?

Or because they were getting too close to the truth?

He could take care of himself. But what about Phoebe? Her instincts weren't honed. Her nature wasn't base. She had no chance against someone with a sick, twisted mind.

The very someone who'd murdered their siblings?

A series of splashes followed by a frustrated *thunk*—a kicked log?—alerted him that danger had crept closer than he'd thought.

Simon froze. Waited. Ears attuned.

More splashes…a sigh of metal on metal…an engine purring to life.

Suddenly the area ahead pulsed with light, sending night creatures fleeing in every direction.

Simon himself squinted against the unnatural brightness, damning the fact that he wasn't close enough to get a good look at the vehicle. When it edged back and veered off in the opposing direction, he let go a breath he hadn't realized he'd been holding.

His first thought was that Phoebe was safe.

For now

Danger—real danger—put an edge to the moment that's difficult to describe.

We were being followed. Even Boone couldn't deny it any longer. My heart hammered when his moment of realization gelled and he jammed the accelerator to the floor. We did some pretty fancy maneuvering around the handful of moving vehicles that stood between us and total privacy.

I stared out the back window and watched the one trying to follow. The distance between us widened....

Boone finally lost our tail down some godforsaken road in the middle of the Glades. Brought me to a place that was at once scary and seductive.

Wild, like our lovemaking.

Even in the midst of a swamp I felt as if prying eyes were on us. My imagination? Perhaps. The sensation added fuel to my desire.

So hot...so humid....

Boone couldn't wait to get inside the house. Right there on the dock, he licked the trails of salty sweat from the hollow of my throat...from the valley between my breasts...from the dip of my navel....

He used his teeth to untie my shorts and tugged the waistband to my hips...would have exposed me and tasted me right there for all his swamp creatures to see....

But who else?

Something stopped me from letting him have his way this time. Impossible to sort out what exactly troubled me.

Instinct?

Awareness?

Imagination?

Unable to shake the distraction, I resisted until after I seduced him inside....

An ominous splash to her left jerked Phoebe out of the reverie. Seeking a safe place, her mind had wandered to equally treacherous territory—an entry in Audra's diary that she'd read earlier that evening.

Was that really a long, large body she heard moving low through the water?

Another splash followed. And another.

Gators on the hunt?

"Breathe easy." The words made her start.

"Simon!" How had he got there? Phoebe wondered if he could really move in utter silence or whether she hadn't heard his approach because she'd been too focused on those scary sounds.

"Whoever it was gave up."

"For now."

"Good enough to get us out of here."

"How?"

"We cut across there," he said, pointing in the direction of the menacing splashes. "And I can borrow an airboat that'll get us to my camp in another five minutes."

"That way is gator territory."

"Uh-huh."

"I *heard* them."

"And your point is? You want to stay here, married to that tree until daybreak?"

"I just don't want to trade one danger for another."

"You're with me now."

And that was *another danger...*

"Stick close," Simon told her. "There are some tricky areas around here."

"Tricky how?"

"False bottom."

Alarmed, she murmured, "Quicksand?"

"Same principle," he said.

Making Phoebe envision taking a wrong step and being swallowed whole.

As they picked their way carefully through more wetlands, Simon kept away from the water and clear land areas and led her across clumps of growth that assured them of solid footing. Staying close to his side, Phoebe felt simultaneously safe and edgy at his very proximity.

Once more she was reminded of the diary entry.

The circumstances of what she'd read were so similar to what they had just experienced, with some unknown person after them, and so similar to what they were experiencing now—taking refuge in unfamiliar territory—that she was finding it more and more difficult to be at ease.

And Simon was like Boone, more than she'd first believed, making her wonder what had closed him off and kept the brothers apart.

Yet, although she and Audra had remained close through thick and thin, *she* wasn't a bit like her sister, Phoebe assured herself. She'd always prided herself on being more evolved. Even if she was attracted to Simon, she could control her own emotions, and keep whatever might happen between them strictly physical. Not get all caught up in living for another person, who in the end would be sure to disappoint her.

A hissing followed by the snap of large jaws jolted her out of her thoughts and into grabbing Simon's arm. "You did hear that, right?"

"Yeah." He was so matter-of-fact that she imagined the sound must be commonplace to him.

"So you're not afraid of alligators?"

"No reason to be."

"I hope you're right," she muttered, edgy despite his confidence. "They have been known to snack on human flesh before."

"When they've been provoked," he agreed. "If they feel threatened they're bound to strike out. But I have a healthy respect for them. And I doubt that human beings are pleasing to their palate."

"What about that toddler last winter?"

"Tragic, but also highly unusual. Without witnesses, we don't know the true circumstances around the attack. The mother didn't go looking for the kid until after he'd vanished.'' He added, ''Besides, a three-year-old is prey-size, while you'd make more than a delectable mouthful...even when that mouth is a foot or so long.''

Annoyed by his obvious amusement over the creeping paranoia she couldn't control, Phoebe asked, ''Isn't there anything you are afraid of?''

For a moment she didn't think he was going to answer.

''More than I like to admit even to myself,'' he said, any touch of good humor gone.

His seriousness sobered her, reminded her of their first meeting.

Though curious, Phoebe kept her questions to herself. She didn't know how, but she'd gotten to Simon on a deeper level than she chose to explore.

The opportunity was soon lost.

They arrived at Simon's intended destination—a building little bigger or fancier than a shack and a small dock in the middle of nowhere, it seemed. There were no lights except the moonlight. No sign of people.

And no airboat, she noted with dismay.

Obviously, whoever Simon had intended to borrow the craft from had gone off somewhere with the hoped-for transportation. Her spirits sank lower.

''So what do we do now?'' she asked, facing her own exhaustion. ''Wait or walk?''

''Wait?''

''For the owner to return.''

''You'd be waiting forever, then.''

A sense of déjà vu jolted Phoebe into making a more thorough examination of their surroundings. The ramshackle place reminded her of...what? She concentrated. Stared harder. Then it came to her. The photograph!

"This was Boone's place?"

"And our mother's before that."

Boone holding Audra here on the landing.

Phoebe could visualize the photo. And something more. The diary passage...

Boone seducing her sister here, on this very spot.

Goose bumps rose along her flesh and Phoebe couldn't rub them away. Weird.

Too weird?

And then it struck her. Surely Simon had recognized the setting of the photo he'd shown her. Why hadn't he said anything about it?

Intending to find out, she said, "Simon..." before realizing the man had wandered off somewhere and had disappeared from her view. Her heart tripped a beat. "Simon!" she called, louder this time.

"Stay there," he returned from some distance.

Still she couldn't see him.

She stared at the shadowed building that had belonged to Simon's brother and to their mother before him. How long before? The place was quite old. Could it have been home to the twins while growing up?

An engine suddenly roared to life, sending night creatures, and Phoebe's pulse, scurrying. She whirled toward the blast as an airboat slid from behind a thicket, but to her relief, it was Simon in the driver's seat. He edged the small craft around a curve, took his foot off the accelerator and cut the power to the battery. The huge caged propeller behind him slowed and he jumped down from his perch to catch onto a rickety post which enabled him to stop the boat.

She'd never piloted one of the shallow-hulled airboats herself, but Phoebe had done enough traveling in them around the Glades, both in water and over the saw grass, enough to know that they were simple-operation vehicles powered by airplane engines. Equipped with battery, accelerator, and rudder, they had no braking mechanism. Guides in the Everglades loved to thrill—and soak—tourists by yanking on the rudder, thereby spinning them to a careening and watery stop.

"Take my hand," Simon said, reaching for her.

Phoebe did so and scrambled into the hull and onto the bench seat that was barely large enough to hold two people.

"Why didn't you tell me about the photo?" she asked before noting he was wearing what looked like thickly padded rubber earmuffs.

Simon's ear-coverings would combat the noise of the engine...and deafen him to her question. It could wait. He handed her a second set and climbed onto the high driver's seat behind her. She barely had the protection in place before the engine thundered to life once more.

They zoomed across open water and then approached a densely overgrown area of mangrove thickets.

And in the water itself, moonlight licked the long, dark backs of creatures that on first glance appeared to be nothing more dangerous than floating logs. A snap of jaws and a foamy splash proved otherwise. One of the gators had caught himself a late-night snack.

Phoebe took a deep breath and looked toward an opening in the tangle of mangrove ahead. Simon headed the airboat straight for the narrow channel.

She'd been in these constricted mazes before, but never at night. The twisted growth closed around and above her like a tapering tunnel. They turned from one channel to another, which was even more confining. Just when she started feeling claustrophobic, Simon angled them out into a wider waterway, then into open water.

A moment later, he torqued the boat to the right and cut the engine. The craft slid sideways with a moderate spray of water before slowing and sliding into a pier. They stopped neatly behind a pair of similar craft.

Phoebe was removing her headset when he jumped down and secured a line. She stepped out of the boat, gaze fixed on the attractive if modest building before them.

The traditional Florida home had been built on stilts. Moon-silvered crushed shell gleamed out at her from the flat surface below the building. No doubt where Simon parked his truck.

When he had a truck to park, she added ruefully.

The house itself was rectangular, constructed of well-weathered wood and a tin roof, and surrounded by natural subtropical growth. The second floor was fronted by a screened-in porch along the entire width of the living quarters. Cultivated vines and flowers dripped from boxes secured along a ledge.

"It's home...the best I could do."

Which made her wonder if he'd built the house himself.

"It's very nice," she said in all honesty.

"Go on in." He indicated the steps on the other side of the building rather than the stairs closer to them and the water. "It's open. Light switch to your left. I'll be right up."

Glad for the opportunity of a few moments alone, Phoebe took him up on the invitation.

She wanted to pull herself together, to decide what direction the rest of the night would take. Sleeping in the same house with Simon....

Or maybe in the same bed.

Chapter Nine

Phoebe charged up the back stairs.

A racing pulse for one reason or another seemed to have become natural to her since she'd met Simon, she thought ruefully.

Danger and desire...different and yet the same in effect.

Could it be that one prompted the other? That, under normal circumstances, she wouldn't have been attracted to Simon at all?

Opening the door, Phoebe switched on the light that illuminated the kitchen area. The interior was simple, with a main room taking up the center half, doors leading to a narrower room on either side, so all three faced the porch and the view beyond.

The practical ceramic tile flooring in a pale shade that reminded her of a blush was scattered with colorful area rugs. The furniture was sparse, of heavy wood and equally colorful cushions. Strategically placed plants natural to the Glades, including several bromeliads and orchids, brought the outdoors inside.

She inhaled the natural fragrance and was stirred anew.

Simple and yet sensual.

Unexpected and yet not.

Simon Calderon...who would have thought?... certainly not she.

How long ago had they met? Forty-eight hours? Two days, and he filled her thoughts...affected her in ways she hadn't before experienced.

The double doors to the screened porch stood open, so she stepped out to take a breath. And to see what was taking Simon so long. Her entrance prompted a clanking and fluttering to her left.

Startled by the bizarre ruckus, she called out, "Simon?"

"Simon says no! Simon says no! Awwwk!"

A parrot!

Her eyes readjusting to the dark, she could see that one full third of the porch had been further screened in to make a huge birdcage. Several perches of natural log had been set at different levels among more plants. Squinting, she made out two similar shadows inside. Macaws.

She drew closer. "Hey, there—"

"Simon says no!" the bird repeated.

Grinning, Phoebe murmured, "Don't I know it. What's your name?"

"That's Mouthy Minerva," came a more familiar voice from directly behind. Simon had caught up to her. "The other one is Shy Serena."

Pulse speeding up, she glanced back at him. "You've managed to give them a splendid home."

"A splendid *cage,*" he countered flatly. "Not that they belong in one."

"If you feel that way, then why did you buy them?"

"I didn't. Got them from a rescue organization. Their original owners were neglecting them to the point of abuse. They couldn't survive on their own," he said, opening a human-sized screen door and stepping inside the cage. "And they're very dependent on human companionship."

As if to prove his words, both macaws ruffled their feathers and moved closer for attention.

"Bedtime, girls."

"Simon says no!" Minerva protested. "Awwwk!"

"Simon says yes," he countered.

A fascinated Phoebe watched as he gave both birds treats from his jeans pockets, then gently stroked their heads and necks. Serena boldly perched on his shoulder and picked at his hair as he moved around the room-sized cage. The bizarre sight brought an unexpected grin to her lips. He was lowering the bamboo roll-up shades, giving the birds the extra incentive they needed to sleep. Minerva followed, hopping from one perch to another, squawking at him and appearing every bit the protesting little kid.

"Yes, it's bedtime," Simon said more firmly, setting Serena on a perch and running his fingers along her neck, then did the same with Minerva. "Good night, girls."

"Awwk, Simon says good night!"

Feeling a new respect for the man, Phoebe said, "You're terrific with them."

"Someone needs to be. They're just a couple more helpless creatures who didn't deserve to be treated badly."

The fervor in his tone got to Phoebe, made her wonder if he was only talking about these birds.

...a couple more helpless creatures... How many had he encountered in his life?

Wanting to know more about him, she asked, "So did you rescue animals as a kid?"

"Sometimes."

"Any of them make good pets?"

"Not for long." Leaving the cage, he secured the door. "My old man had no use for animals except for the money they could provide him. Never had any respect for their lives." His tone bitter, he said, "Then again, he had no respect for human beings, either, not even for his own family."

"Parents can be difficult," Phoebe admitted. "It wasn't until my dad knew he was dying that he tried to have a real relationship with me."

Simon crossed in front of her to the screened wall, where he stared out at the swamp. He stood there, silent, arms crossed over his chest. And Phoebe figured he was closing himself off again.

So when he said, "My old man died hating us...Boone and me," she was shocked.

And what an awful thing for him to believe. "I'm sure he didn't hate his own sons."

"How could he not? We were responsible for his death."

Back still to her, Simon spoke tonelessly, but

Phoebe sensed the smoldering emotions beneath the calm surface.

Certain Boone had said something about their father dying when they were kids, she asked, "How old were you?"

"Nearly twelve."

"Kind of young to take on such a terrific responsibility."

"Boone and I were always old beyond our years, as far back as I can remember. We had to be...for our mother's sake." Simon faltered, making her think he wasn't going to discuss it further, then said, "He was the worst kind of abuser."

Phoebe closed her eyes and swallowed hard. For as much grief as she'd felt over her mother and Audra being mentally abused by men they'd loved, she'd never had to face bruises or broken bones, and she was certain that's what he meant.

Moving closer to Simon, she placed a sympathetic hand on his shoulder. "I'm sorry."

"*He* never was."

Even with nothing more than the moon illuminating the porch, she could see enough of his face to know that his jaw was working. Because he wanted to say more? Or was he clenching it against the memory?

"It was always Mama's fault." His voice turned rough. Edgy. "His losing a job...getting drunk... losing his temper. The old man always put it on her...sometimes with both fists."

Her stomach clenched at the image that conjured

up. "That had to be tough on a couple of helpless kids."

"We tried to stop him, but he only beat her worse, until we stopped him for good."

The night suddenly closed in on Phoebe. Dear God, she was starting to wonder what he'd meant by his and Boone being responsible for their father's death. Surely nothing literal, though...

Finding it hard to breathe normally, she whispered, "What happened?"

Again, he didn't jump to clue her in. Of course he was reluctant. The memories had to be painful. But she was certain he wanted her to know or he would never have let the conversation go this far. He was opening up.

Why?

Even as she wondered, Simon started slowly. "He didn't like the way Mama made the chicken that night. Too spicy, he told her, made his gut ache. More likely it was his damn liver rotting from all the booze..." Expressionless, he met her gaze. "He threw the bowl at her."

Without planning it, Phoebe reached out and slipped her fingers into his. His hand closed around hers.

"Mama tried ducking, but it hit the side of her head. I thought she was going to pass out. Blood was trickling down her cheek...he ordered her to pick up every last piece of chicken off the floor. When she wasn't moving fast enough for his liking...she was so stunned, she couldn't...he slapped her until she did."

His grip tightened, but Phoebe didn't resist. Her sympathy went out to him in a return squeeze.

"And like always," Simon continued, "he said he was doing it because he loved her so much he had to correct her, for her own good, of course. Always for her own good."

"How awful," Phoebe murmured, only wishing there were some way she could take away the hurt that still had so much power over him.

His admission got to her in a way for which she wasn't prepared. It felt...personal. She remembered hearing Vance say something similar to Audra once...

Could he have been physically abusing her sister without her knowing?

"He was out of work again," Simon went on, as if she wasn't even there, "picking up money where he could. Later that night, he decided to go frogging. He sold frogs by the pound to a local restaurant. And he made us help, Boone and me. We were so angry, we didn't want to go with him that night. We never should have, but we were afraid he'd take out his temper on Mama again."

"So what happened?" she asked, a knot in her stomach. "An accident?"

When he shook his head, the knot tightened.

"We were out hunting in the grasslands. Neither of us would speak to him. We caught frogs, put them in the bucket...but we wouldn't answer when he asked us something. The silent treatment got to the old man 'cause he was feeling guilty, I guess. He started criticizing. Told Boone he wasn't handling his gigging pole right. And then Boone just exploded. He couldn't keep it back anymore. Not the anger, not the hatred that gets all mixed up with the love you want to feel… He asked the old man what he was going to do to teach him different, asked if he was he going to hit him like he had Mama…''

Phoebe's heart faltered. "Did he?"

"He tried. He was furious. He came at Boone and Boone used his gigging pole to keep the old man at a distance. He shoved him real hard. The alcohol was still affecting him. The old man wasn't what you would call steady on his feet even on a good day. He lost his balance and took a couple of clumsy steps back off the grassland and straight into the water…''

Not waiting for him to find the words, Phoebe asked, "So he what? Drowned?"

Simon shook his head. "False bottom. He started to sink. I was frozen. I watched him scrabble for something to hold on to. Some branch or root—something he could use to pull himself back out. Nothing held.''

Like the area he'd warned her about earlier, Phoebe thought, wondering if he knew every questionable inch of the Glades, or if that particular spot held these terrible, personal memories.

"The old man just kept scrabbling and sinking," Simon was saying. "Then he started swearing…and begging and a little voice inside me told me to stay put, that doing nothing would stop his hurting Mama. I was tempted, Phoebe, I admit it. I wanted to stay put, only I couldn't. I tried to get to him…''

"But it was too late?"

"Boone stopped me." His words floored her. "He was out of control, all wide-eyed and yelling that he loved the old man so much he was gonna teach *him* a lesson...just like the ones Mama got. I tried to get by him, but he shoved me down and held me there...insisted it had to be this way to make sure she was safe. I tried to tell him it wasn't right, but he was past listening. I had to fight my way back up, but then it was too late."

Horrified, Phoebe could only imagine what it must be like to watch anyone die, let alone a parent. That had to have been devastating for Simon, even if his father had been a drunkard and an abuser, a man whose sickness had infected his son...

But only for that brief moment in the Glades, she assured herself, hoping to God she hadn't been wrong about Boone.

"Odd that the authorities never brought up his untimely death," she mused. "If they had..."

"If they had, what? Would you have believed their theory about Boone?"

Simon ran his knuckles down the side of her face. Affected by the gesture that was gentle and affectionate, pressing her cheek into his fingers, Phoebe swayed toward him.

"Maybe," she murmured.

"Phoebe, with the heart too pure to suspect the worst in human nature, would take as gospel some unspeakable accusation she couldn't prove for herself? Now that I don't believe."

"You make me sound hopelessly naive."

"Aren't you?" His fingertips worked their way beneath her hair, to stroke her neck. "Not that it's a bad thing."

Suddenly finding it difficult to keep track of the conversation, she murmured, "It isn't?"

He shook his head. "It's refreshing to know the world hasn't tainted all its innocents."

"Watch who you call innocent," she protested.

He touched her cheek, and for the merest whisper of time, she suspected he would kiss her. She *wanted* him to kiss her...and more.

"As for the authorities," he continued softly, his face drawing nearer to hers, "they didn't bring up the old man's death because they didn't know. People disappear in the Glades from time to time, casualties of an uncivilized land. No one even questioned our story."

So he'd lied to cover for Boone, Phoebe realized. She could imagine that hadn't been easy for a twelve-year-old who'd had torn feelings about his father. And the lie must have preyed on his mind for years. Maybe still did.

She covered the hand cupping her cheek, and it was as if she were electrified by the contact. "But your mother—"

"Went to her grave believing she'd lost her husband to an accident. And Boone and I never spoke of the true nature of that night again. Hell, I've never spoken about it to anyone. Until now."

And why to her? Phoebe wondered again. At least now she understood Simon's initial attitude in accepting the murder-suicide theory.

"No wonder you were so ready to believe your

own brother was a murderer. You'd seen a violent side of Boone that no one else even suspected.''

''And I couldn't tell you then.''

''Why me?'' she finally asked aloud. ''Why now?''

''We shared something tonight...a brush with death. Two people can't get closer than that.''

''Yes, they can,'' she said, wanting to do just that. Perhaps he could find comfort in her arms. Better yet, they could find comfort in each other. Someone had been after them. Had tried to hurt them. Maybe worse.

That's all it was, she told herself as she slipped her arms up around his neck as if it were the most natural thing in the world for her to do. Need. Comfort. And fulfillment of the natural urges that had been plaguing her since she'd met Simon Calderon.

Natural urges intensified by reading passages from Audra's diary...

His face was so close now she could hardly focus on it. But she could see that his lids drooped. She concentrated on his sexy bedroom eyes rather than on what had almost happened to them earlier.

What she read there sent her pulse skittering.

She lifted her face in invitation.

''Why, Phoebe,'' Simon murmured, ''I believe you are trying to seduce me.''

''What if I am?'' she asked breathlessly, her world suddenly narrowing to the two of them.

''Then I'm flattered. And curious.''

''About what?''

''Why?''

''I need a reason?'' A blush started from her middle, warmed her already sensitive breasts and crept up to her face. No man had ever expected her to explain a need as natural as breathing before. "How about…we can take comfort in each other's arms," she said lightly.

"That's it?"

He didn't try to hide his amusement. Did he really have to tease her now? Senses heightened, she was in the mood for physical rather than verbal satisfaction.

"We are attracted to each other, right?" Surely she couldn't be mistaken about something so basic.

"I am attracted to you, yes," he admitted.

"Well, then…"

Before he could grill her further, Phoebe decided to take the situation into her own hands.

Rather her lips…

Rising on tiptoe, she found his mouth. At first he seemed as if he were going to resist, but then his lips softened. Opened. Invited her in.

The raw sound escaping his throat thrilled her. The sound of a man in lust…with her.

Set aflame, Phoebe was gratified by his arms snaking around her waist, drawing her closer. Tighter.

She was trembling. Willing.

Wanting Simon Calderon more than any man she'd ever known.

Wanting to burn away unpleasant thoughts and memories; the shock of someone trying to kill them.

She pressed herself into him and rocked her hips until her lower body fit his perfectly. He cupped her derriere and groaned again. Flushed with desire, she raised a knee and slid her leg around his.

His readiness pressed against her belly...he could take her right there.

And she was certain he would.

She *hoped* he would...

His hand slid down and around her bottom along the underside of her leg and toward her center. His initial foray elicited from her an intense response and slicked her inner flesh with a wet warmth she was anxious for him to explore further.

Through the soft cotton of her trousers, his long fingers traced the elastic of her lace panties. Then he swept straight to the heart of her femininity, the thin layers of material presenting no barrier to sensation. Lifting her leg higher, she opened herself and pushed into the seduction of his touch.

He cupped her, stroked her, invaded her as far as the garment would allow.

Not enough...not nearly enough...

When he left a trail of sensual bites down the length of her neck, she gasped and dug her nails into his shoulders, silently urging him to take her higher.

He found a rhythm, coaxed another flow from her until the material between her thighs dampened with her essence. She was sure he could feel it, wanted him to. Every inch of her flesh had been awakened and every nerve was singing. Her breasts swelled and ached. And she felt her own pulse race in the most intimate of places.

Desperate for more pleasure, wanting the same for him, she slid a hand between them and found him equally aroused. Not satisfied, she forced her way beneath his jeans and along his naked flesh.

Better.

His flesh was hot. Vibrant. Responsive.

She trailed the tips of her nails along his smooth length and used her forefinger to circle his tip. His sharp intake of breath intensified her need.

Suddenly his hands loosened their grip...

Finding her shoulders and setting her from him...

So he wouldn't take her right there, after all, Phoebe realized, his lack of spontaneity disappointing but certainly not killing the mood. Perhaps a bed would better the first time, anyway.

Eager to get there, to finish what she'd started, she didn't understand why he wasn't moving.

Then, on a shaky breath, he asked, "What else, Phoebe? Why do you want to be with me?"

Startled, she stared through the dark. He was turned away from the moon so his expression was hidden from her.

Why in the world was he questioning her again?

Something about his tone sounded wrong. So serious. Needy in a way that scared the stuffing out of her.

Her desire dimmed, but she didn't give up yet.

"What is it you want me to say, Simon?" She tried to keep her words light, flirtatious, but she feared escalating tension of another sort was pouring out of her with every syllable. "Surely you're not the one man in the world who needs assurances before having sex."

"Sex. Right." Now it was he who sounded disappointed. "Soft words from your lips would be

nice,'' he agreed. ''Some sentiment beyond the physical.''

He *did* want assurances!

Internal alarms going off, Phoebe backed away
from the man and wrapped her arms around her middle. The last of her ardor cooled as quickly as it had
been aroused.

''Why do we have to talk at all?'' she asked, wishing she could be anywhere else in the world.

''It's what people do when they get close.''

Close?

Positive he didn't mean it in the physical sense, she
wondered how *close* he wanted to get.

She snapped, ''Men say pretty words far too easily,
and just as easily do ugly things to the very women
they're supposed to—care about.''

She couldn't even say the word *love.* Not when she
didn't believe in it.

''They do, don't they?'' He sounded as distant as
she was beginning to feel.

Making Phoebe start.

And recognize the tension radiating from *him.*

Anger? Hurt?

But why?

And then a thought struck her.

Surely Simon didn't believe she was referring to
his parents. He had, after all, just told her that his
father had hit his mother while vowing his love. In
truth, she'd been referring to the parade of men her
mother had ushered through her life.

''Simon, I think you've got the wrong idea—''

''You don't have a clue as to what goes on inside

my head," he growled, sweeping by her and into the house.

"Simon!" She followed. "Let me explain."

But it was too late.

He stopped and faced her, any ardor he'd been feeling seemingly gone if his expression was any indication. His gaze swept over her as impersonally as if she were nothing more than an acquaintance.

"Talk about bringing the outdoors inside."

Phoebe glanced down at the muck that clung to her from their run through the swamp. What a mess! Simon looked equally grubby and she was sure he knew it. His defense mechanisms were up and he was striking out, attempting to embarrass her.

For once, she couldn't think of a thing to say, clever or otherwise.

When she didn't respond, he said, "You can have the shower all to yourself. You'll find fresh towels and a robe in the bathroom closet."

At a loss to know how to fix this, she finally found her voice. "I guess I should just leave my clothes on and do my laundry at the same time, huh?"

But her attempt at humor fell flat. Simon was already halfway toward the door.

And Phoebe watched him storm out, the weirdest longing welling up in her.

She wanted to stop him. To say whatever it would take to get him to come back.

To make things right between them.

The lump in her throat nearly choked her.

She wanted...

What?

Nothing, she assured herself firmly. All along she'd known Simon Calderon was the wrong man to lust after. He wasn't casual and easy to talk to. He wasn't like any other man she'd ever been with. From the first hint of attraction, she'd known she couldn't control the situation, so why had she started anything in the first place?

And why the disappointment when she'd merely proved herself correct?

Heading for the shower, Phoebe had never felt so miserable.

All hint of physical desire had vanished, and yet she was left wanting something she couldn't name.

A COLD SHOWER should fix what ailed him, but Simon found the stinging water invigorating to his perfectly healthy libido. He might have stopped himself from taking Phoebe, but that didn't stop him from wanting her.

Standing naked under the simple outdoor shower he'd installed beneath the bathroom, he soaped himself vigorously, as if he could wash away the effect she was still having on him. But that only made him think of her doing the same directly overhead.

Phoebe touching herself, running her fingers through the soap...

Once the image came to him, it was firmly planted in his mind.

He ought to have his head examined.

Passing up what Phoebe had offered...what had gotten into him?

Over the past couple of days, he'd imagined taking

her more times than he cared to admit. The adrenaline rush that had followed their escape had prompted the perfect opportunity. And he'd blown it by pressing her, trying to make her say something she obviously wasn't feeling.

He'd never done that before.

Not with any other woman.

He'd reacted too quickly. Too strongly.

He never should have delved into the past in the first place.

What had been his point?

Why had he revealed the worst moments of his life to this particular woman? Why Phoebe?

What made her so special?

And why couldn't he free himself of the image of her all soapy and wet, her fingers threading through the foam laving her flesh…touching herself in the most intimate of places even as he longed to do?

Chapter Ten

"Why didn't you say something about owning a telephone last night?"

Phoebe had held back the complaint through an awkward breakfast—not that Simon's appetite had suffered in the least. Great. Any embarrassment over last night's events was strictly on her side, and she had enough for both of them.

They were heading down the rear stairs on their way to the airboat, which they would take back to his childhood home. There they would trade it for an ancient pickup, which, he assured her, would run with a little coaxing. Then he would return her to the Blue Crab and her car.

Having called his local service station first thing that morning about getting a tow and new tires, Simon had been assured his own vehicle would be ready in several hours. Phoebe hadn't wanted to hang around that long. Being alone with him was too unnerving.

"I could have called that taxi," she grumbled as they hit ground level. "Or better yet, you could have driven me back to Marco last night in the pickup you didn't bother to mention along with the phone."

Which would have saved her from making a fool of herself. At least he had the decency to avoid mentioning it. Phoebe counted her blessings.

"You would have gone home to an empty house," he said.

"I usually do."

A fact that had never bothered her before. She loved her house. The first place she'd ever lived in that she could call home and mean it. Suddenly it loomed empty and lonely in her mind.

Maybe she ought to get a pet. Another Mouthy Minerva to keep her company.

"You don't usually have someone try to run you over with a four-by-four," Simon was saying.

"But Bubba doesn't know where I live."

"You don't know that for sure."

She'd already called the authorities to report the incident. She'd spoken to Detective Sandstrom, the man handling Boone and Audra's case. However, he wasn't ready to believe there was a connection between their deaths and the attempt on her and Simon.

Yet.

At least she'd planted a seed in his mind, Phoebe thought.

"Detective Sandstrom promised they would find Bubba and pick him up as soon as possible for questioning. They could have done that last night."

"What if Bubba isn't the one who tried to kill us?"

"We've already been through this."

Though she'd considered the possibility that Vance

had been the one behind the wheel, she didn't think it likely. He would have had to follow them from the Blue Crab, and surely Simon would have spotted a tail. More likely Bubba had called Vance to warn him they were buying information…and her brother-in-law had paid the man to do his dirty work.

Getting herself into the airboat was a welcome distraction from her dark thoughts. And she was glad enough to put on the extra headset so she wouldn't have to carry on any further conversation with Simon, who seemed to be in surprisingly good spirits.

Feeling his gaze on her, she ignored him and pretended interest in the local flora. Aware of his every movement, she knew the exact moment he took the raised seat behind her. She settled in even as the engine roared to life. A moment later, they were on the move.

All through the night, she'd tossed and turned, too aware of Simon sacked out on the couch to get herself a good night's sleep. He, on the other hand, had seemed amazingly well rested over breakfast. No wonder, considering the amount of snoring she'd been subjected to.

Hadn't what almost happened between them affected him at all?

As they raced along, the amazingly clear morning and still comfortable air relaxed her a bit. She spotted a couple of raccoons fishing at the shoreline, a turtle sunning itself on a log, and an osprey floating on a draft overhead. Not an alligator in sight. With the sun's rise, the swamp had lost its threat. She could even wonder at her own imagination.

What had gotten into her the night before?

A few minutes later, they docked. Simon jumped down from his seat and tied up the boat. Reluctantly, knowing she'd have no choice but to talk to him, Phoebe removed the padded headsets that had served as protection from him as well as from the engine's noise.

"It might take a little coaxing to get the pickup running," he said. "Why don't you go on inside until I do."

Of course he didn't really want to talk to her, either. His good humor had been a front.

"Sure, I'll be happy to get out of your hair," she muttered.

"Phoebe—"

She turned her back to him and kept going.

Sunlight dappling across Simon's childhood home gave it a certain charm that had been lacking in the middle of the night. And the inside, while small, was inviting.

Enough bright light shone through the windows to make the pale yellow walls glow. The furniture might be old, but it appeared well-tended. While she wasn't into furnishing her place with antiques, she recognized the potential value of some pieces. No doubt they were original to the house, but they looked as if they'd been restored.

Rag rugs hid part of what looked to be a new wood floor, one Phoebe guessed to be of a modern material that would hold up against the elements instead. Boone's doing, no doubt.

Because he'd wanted the place as a private love nest?

Curious, she entered the bedroom whose door stood open.

The full-sized bed had a metal headboard and was covered by a hand-sewn quilt.

Wondering if Simon's mother had made it, she perched on the edge of the mattress and admired the handmade piece up close. She'd barely gotten a look when a blast of a horn alerted her to Simon's success with the old pickup.

Rising, she hesitated when something out of place caught her eye—a small object that had fallen between bed and nightstand. It looked to be a figure of some sort.

The horn blew again, conveying Simon's impatience.

Deciding he could wait a moment longer, she retrieved the fallen object, the figure of a woman. Attached to the small doll were a lock of blond hair and a piece of cloth whose leafy pattern looked familiar.

She'd bought her sister a scarf with this very same pattern several months before, after Audra had admired it in an exclusive Old Naples shop...but Audra had only worn it once before losing it.

Or had she lost it, after all?

Phoebe caught her breath when she realized the pins attaching the cloth to the figure were stuck in strategic places—sexual regions, in addition to the heart and the middle of the forehead.

Her sister had been shot in the head...and a crime of passion involved the others.

Her own heart began to pound and for once it had nothing to do with danger to herself or Simon.

The county authorities lacked proof that anyone other than Boone might have wanted her sister dead. What if she held that proof in her hand?

What if someone had created a voodoo doll in her sister's image, as a warning, or to foreshadow the evil deed!

WHAT IN THE WORLD was taking Phoebe so long? Simon wondered as the old pickup shook and rattled.

He blew the horn a third time, again to no response. Afraid that if he cut the engine he might not be able to get the damn thing running again, and that if he *didn't* cut the engine they might run out of gas, he was getting angry. Figuring he'd better see what was hanging her up for himself, he decided to chance the gas.

A moment later, he burst through the front door, yelling, "Hey, Phoebe, I thought you were in a hurry to get home!"

He didn't see her at first. Anxious, he whipped around, momentarily thinking something had happened to her. And then he spotted the open bedroom door.

"Phoebe, are you in there?"

She was sitting on the bed, staring at something in her hand. Her face was pale, her eyes huge. She appeared at once frightened and elated. For a moment, she stared straight at him without seeming to realize he was there.

Then she blinked, jumped up from the bed and waved something at him. "Look at this."

"What is it?"

"See for yourself."

Expectancy radiated from her as Phoebe hurried to show him the small object.

Carefully examining the figure, which a more superstitious person than he would believe had the power to kill someone, Simon frowned. "Where did you find this?"

She indicated the area between bed and nightstand. "It must have fallen."

Simon splayed the lock of hair with a fingertip. "Blond. Wasn't Audra—"

Phoebe jumped in with, "That's her hair, all right."

"Can you be certain?"

"Not without scientific testing, I guess. But trust me, it's as close a color and texture match as you could get. I definitely can identify the material, because it's a piece of a scarf I gave her."

"Someone could have stolen the scarf or even picked it up if she left it behind somewhere," Simon mused, "but hair's another matter."

"Women do change hairstyles," Phoebe insisted. "And Audra had hers cut several weeks ago. I was surprised she'd gone so much shorter. She said the longer hair was more trouble than it was worth, especially during the summer, but Vance had always insisted she keep it that way. I guess she saw the change as another shot at cutting herself loose from him. And since he was having her followed…"

"Whoa." He could tell where she was going with this and he couldn't buy it. "Can you really see Bubba going inside some posh hair salon to spy on Audra, without making a spectacle of himself?—and somehow managing to abscond with a lock of her hair?"

Phoebe's brow pulled. "Kind of hard to imagine when you put it that way."

"And has Vance ever given you any clue that he's into the black arts?"

"Well, no, but—"

"So this isn't proof of anything, just gives us something more to think about."

"And something to check on," she added. "Audra and I went to the same hairstylist. I can ask David if anything weird happened that day."

"If he can remember that far back."

"And I wonder what Detective Sandstrom would make of something so hateful."

"What would be the point in telling him now?"

"What do you mean?"

"We have no idea where the doll came from, so you can't suggest a new suspect. Besides, it's a little unusual for the purveyor of evil to send the supposed means of death to the victim," Simon went on logically, "and you found the doll in here—in a house that my brother owned. Who would have better access to a scarf your sister wore than her lover? Or better access to her hair? He could have snipped off a lock while she slept. You'd only be pointing a finger back at him."

Phoebe couldn't deny it. And when she asked, "Do *you* believe that?" her voice was hollow. Resigned.

"No, not after last night. But if you'd put it to me two days ago?" He shrugged. No doubt he would have thought the worst, which he'd been primed to do. And that would have given him yet another reason to suspect his own dark side. Oddly enough, Simon felt his self-doubts receding.

Phoebe appeared crestfallen and Simon regretted that he was responsible for her disappointment. Again. She'd had just such a look the night before, when he'd stopped things from going too far between them.

In the cold light of day, he knew he'd done the right thing. Not that the fact made it easier on either of them. After last night, he realized he wanted more than sex from her—a confusing turn of events, considering they hardly knew each other. And if he'd given her what she'd been asking for, they both would have had cause to regret sleeping together, if for different reasons.

Phoebe brightened suddenly. "What about the fingerprints on the doll?"

"The person who made this could have been wearing gloves. But chances are if Boone had his hands on the thing, he wouldn't have taken any kind of precautions. Not any more than we just did."

"So what *do* we do?" Phoebe asked with a sigh.

She appeared so forlorn that Simon couldn't help himself. Meaning to put his arms around her for her comfort, he took a step toward her but stopped in his tracks when she flashed him a deadly glare.

Obviously, she wasn't having any comfort. Not from him. Not today.

He cleared his throat and said, "We hang on to it, for now. And we get you back to Marco. If we don't hurry, we won't make it as far as the nearest gas station."

"And get stuck out here in the middle of the swamp any longer than necessary? No, thanks." She was already swinging past him and on her way out the front door when he heard her say, "Not in my lifetime."

Simon narrowed his gaze and followed, muttering too low for her to hear. "We'll see about that, Phoebe Grant. We'll just see about that."

PHOEBE WOULD HAVE GONE straight to Dolphin's Gate to check on Jimmy Bob Dortch, as she'd threatened, especially since he'd promised to be there at eight and it was long past that, but home was on the way.

Home...and Audra's diary.

Her sister would never have left out something so sinister as receiving a voodoo doll, and Phoebe meant to discover what she'd written about the curse. Perhaps Audra had even figured out who was responsible.

Besides, her stopping for a few minutes wouldn't make any difference one way or the other to the work that was supposed to be going on in her mother's townhouse. If Jimmy Bob was there, he was there. And if he wasn't...

She would check on him as soon as she satisfied her curiosity.

Pulling into the garage, Phoebe rushed into the house and filched the journal from her nightstand, then threw herself across the bed.

The voodoo doll obviously had to have been made after Audra's haircut, somewhere around the Fourth of July.

Phoebe skipped forward a few weeks in her reading and started skimming until she found an entry that made her sit up and take notice.

The most frightening thing happened to me last night....

What could be more frightening than finding tangible and potentially deadly proof of someone's hatred for you?

With a sense of trepidation, Phoebe settled in to read.

The most frightening thing happened to me last night....

It started ordinary enough. A romantic dinner. A walk along the beach. Foreplay under the moonlight.

But for once, he wasn't so eager to take me on the spot. I did my best to convince him to try, but he was acting a little weird, taunting me with promises of a delicious surprise once he got me into bed.

The silk ties weren't just a surprise...they were a bit of a shock. The idea of his tying me up was titillating. And scary.

What to do?

How much did I trust him?

How much control was I willing to give someone I really hadn't known that long?

Up to you, he whispered, even as he began his seduction. He used all the resources in his very potent arsenal, keeping at me—keeping satisfaction from me—until I had no will to resist left....

Phoebe came up for air. Dropping the diary, she took a shaky breath and fought the yearning that had built in her instantly. Fought the seductive image of Simon that all too readily came to mind. Fought the memories of what had almost happened between them.

Memories that threatened her sense of contentment and security.

But she had to go on reading, no matter the cost to herself. Had to learn what had frightened her sister so badly.

Praying it hadn't been Boone himself, Phoebe steeled herself and once again picked up the record of her sister's last weeks on earth.

He dragged the silk over my naked body. The experience was so luxurious and erotic that my flesh pebbled...and my insides quaked.

I'm not certain when, exactly, the misgiving began, but sometime during this foreplay—maybe after both of my wrists were tied to the headboard and he was winding the third scarf around my ankle—I sensed we were being watched. The impression was no different from the one I'd had out on the street when we'd avoided the other vehicle.

Foolish…stupid.

How could that be in my own bedroom? I *tried* to convince myself…but I couldn't.

Finally, I put the fear into words. He just laughed, teased me about being paranoid, and— securing the fourth scarf—suggested my reaction came from doing something foreign and forbidden.

Naked…spread-eagled…vulnerable…

I tried to believe him.

But I couldn't relax. He was determined to make me. Even as he made love to me, whispering hot, sexy promises of how he would turn me inside out all night, uneasy thoughts raced through my mind.

What if someone really *was* watching?

To my shame, the fear heightened the experience.

I could almost see another set of eyes glued to our every movement, another set of ears hearing our every moan. The imagining of a third person in that room, a party to our lovemaking, did nothing to cool my ardor.

I burned brighter…wanted more intensely…had to have more.…

And in the midst of his bringing me to the pinnacle again and again, another terrible, frightening thought occurred to me. What if I were making it all up because I needed more than

Boone alone could give to satisfy me?
The truth or an imagined necessity....
Which would be worse?

An uneasy Phoebe lowered her sister's journal, for once more disturbed by the contents than by the erotic imaginings it normally produced. As usual, all her senses were heightened, especially that same sixth sense—dread—which had struck Audra so sharply.

Shivering, she gazed into the four corners of her own bedroom, as if expecting someone to be spying on *her*.

Had Audra really recognized a frightening truth that had precipitated her death—or had it merely been sex-play for her like the other times she'd played with Boone?

Erotic games, sex toys, intimate paraphernalia, Audra had been into them all.

Could it be that lust had ruled her sister for so long that she'd needed the extra incentive to be satisfied?

Disturbed by the possibility, and by the parallels she could start drawing to herself, Phoebe stiffly flipped through the remaining pages of the diary, reading nothing, merely picking out words here and there.

No *voodoo doll*.

Thankful to be done with it, she shoved the leather-bound book back into the drawer next to the one she'd found in the shoe box at Vance's place. A glance at the nightstand clock reminded her of her obligations.

If she was going to check on Jimmy Bob Dortch

before reporting for work, she needed to get a move on.

A quick change of clothing and she was on her way.

If she'd been hoping the ride to Dolphin's Gate would settle her down, she was sorely disappointed. Audra's self-doubts had brought up some of her own.

Not that she needed unusual circumstances or games—rather it was that she didn't seem to want *more*.

That fact had bothered Simon so much that he'd rejected her. A somewhat sobering first. Her experience with men, while limited in comparison to that of her mother or Audra, was enough to know that "more" wasn't normally what men were looking for. Those she'd been with had been happy enough to take what she'd offered and hadn't complained when she'd chosen to end the short-term affairs.

Why hadn't that been enough for Simon Calderon?

What made him different?

And why did she care?

Phoebe tried to shake her weird reaction prompted by the journal entry, but as she sailed through the development's entrance, she realized that wasn't as easy as she'd like. She felt that she was coming to some kind of crisis in her life, and that scared her. All wound up, she had as little success as Audra in trying to relax.

Seeing Jimmy Bob's truck in her mother's driveway, Phoebe practically flew from her convertible into her mother's townhouse.

"Jimmy Bob, it's Miss Phoebe," she called.

Expecting to see him at work, she instead faced an empty kitchen. His toolbox lay open on the floor. Materials spread along the counter.

But no Jimmy Bob.

How peculiar.

Pulse fluttering strangely, she stopped and stood listening to the refrigerator hum.

Growing apprehension filled her as she tried again. "Jimmy Bob, where are you?"

Had the handyman wandered off somewhere in search of a forgotten tool?

A thump directly overhead dashed that idea. She considered quickly—the sound had come from Audra's bedroom.

He had no business being anywhere but the kitchen, so what in the world was he up to?

Phoebe crept up the stairs, all the while attuned to the strange noises issuing from the bedroom. She'd swear the handyman was moving furniture.

Just outside the door, she paused and took a deep breath. Then she stepped inside.

Jimmy Bob was standing on an upholstered chair he'd pulled directly to a wall of built-in storage units. The louvered doors to a top cupboard stood open, and he was rooting around inside.

Eyes wide, she demanded, "What the hell do you think you're doing?"

The handyman whipped around, and in trying to maintain his balance, released the object he'd just picked up. It flew directly at her and landed at her feet.

Phoebe stooped to retrieve it.

A video camera.

And a videotape recorder was sitting on the floor next to the chair, while two wires hung from the open section of the wall unit.

She tried to grasp what all this meant and could only come to one conclusion.

"Jimmy Bob, how long were you recording what was going on in my sister's bedroom?"

Chapter Eleven

Averting his gaze from hers, Jimmy Bob whimpered and shifted from one foot to the other. Tufts of light brown hair stuck out from under his billed cap and around his florid face. He looked guilty as sin standing on that chair, and it took all Phoebe's willpower not to scream at him to get down and explain himself immediately.

As calmly as she could manage, she said, "I believe I asked you a question, Jimmy Bob."

"Gotta go."

He practically fell in his haste to scramble down from the chair.

"Not so fast." She planted herself between him and the door. "You have some explaining to do. What are you doing in this room with this equipment?"

And what was the equipment doing there in the first place? A camera lens aimed through the louvers of the cupboard door would give a direct view of the bed. She realized her sister probably never even guessed it existed—Audra hadn't taken enough with her to fill all the storage space, so she'd probably never even opened the high doors. Anyone could have been tracking her sister's sexual activities. Someone who'd been obsessed...

She shuddered at the thought.

"Who is responsible for this?" she demanded. "How did you know about the equipment?"

The handyman jammed his billed cap lower over his forehead. "I'll finish the kitchen, now, Miss Phoebe."

"No! *You* are finished here, for good," she said firmly. No way was she going to give him free rein in the place. No matter the circumstances, he'd taken enough of that already. "Do you understand? You're fired."

"Yes, ma'am."

Despite the evidence, she had a hard time believing that he was responsible for installing video equipment in her sister's bedroom. What would be his purpose? And was he even capable of the concept, let alone the execution?

"If you don't want to talk to me about what you've been doing, Jimmy Bob," she said, desperate to get to whatever truth he could tell her, "then you can give your explanations to the police."

"No police!" His voice rose to a squeak.

Phoebe could tell he was fighting panic. What was he hiding? Who was he trying to protect?

"Who put you up to this?" she demanded, Vance being her first choice.

"No one!" he yelled, trying to get past her.

Her pulse raced as she stood fast. "Maybe the police will ask what else you know about my sister...and about her murder.''

Jimmy Bob instantly became as agitated as he had the morning before at the Blue Crab. Had she struck on some ribbon of truth? Phoebe was ready to throw the camera at him—an improvised weapon—and to run if she had to, but the man made no threatening moves.

''Mr. Boone did it! They said so on the TV!''

''Maybe they were wrong.''

Phoebe knew she was taking a chance baiting him. Even if he was slow, he could be dangerous. Nothing to say he couldn't have killed for money.

''But maybe you already know that,'' she went on. ''Maybe you had something to do with Audra's death.''

His sudden stricken expression surprised Phoebe; she was certain he wasn't faking.

''I would never hurt Miss Audra. Not ever. She was always nice to me.''

''Then why weren't you nice in return?''

''I *was*. And I would never do nothin' wrong. Not to her. I—I l-loved her!''

Phoebe's momentary shock gave the handyman the edge long enough for him to push by her.

''Jimmy Bob, wait!'' She followed him out the door. ''Who put you up to this?''

''I'm leavin' now!'' he yelled, flying down the stairs.

''Was it Vance Laughlin? Audra's husband?''

''You can't stop me!''

Knowing she wasn't going to get an answer out of

him, Phoebe gave up. She stood at the top of the staircase for the moment it took him to cross the living area and run out the door. He didn't even stop long enough to collect his tools.

Outside, his engine started right up and he wheeled his truck out of the drive so fast that his tires squealed.

Leaving Phoebe clutching the camera and wondering whether Jimmy Bob was really as innocent of wrongdoing as he claimed...or if he knew more about her sister's death and who was responsible than he was telling.

WHEN SIMON ARRIVED at Calderon Charters, Corky Slotnik was leaning over Elise's desk, practically drooling on her. She didn't seem to mind. She was smiling and laughing at something he'd said.

Figuring if he was going to be the boss he ought to act like one, Simon cleared his throat. "Glad to see we're all so busy this morning."

Corky's buzz cut practically bristled as he reluctantly straightened and went back to his own desk, muttering, "Ever hear of a coffee break?"

"So where's your coffee?"

Elise, too, had sobered at the sight of him, but rather than being hostile, she seemed almost embarrassed. Her exotic features were drawn, her soft brown eyes avoiding his.

Stopping at her desk, he asked, "Magnus out with a charter this morning?"

Her eyebrows arched. "No. He goes out at noon, though."

Simon checked his watch. Not for an hour, then.

"You need him for something in particular?" she asked.

"I'd just like to get to know him better," he hedged. No need to raise her suspicions. "The other captains, too."

Calderon Charters owned a fleet of two moderate-sized cruisers, six manned fishing boats and an equal number of lesser rental craft. Indeed, Simon did want to get to know his nearly three dozen full- and part-time employees, but that wasn't the purpose of his seeking out Magnus Hanson this morning. Like Elise, the captain had been with his brother from the first, and Simon figured picking the old man's brain couldn't hurt.

The late morning was growing hot as he strolled out of the air-conditioned office and onto the pier. Halfway down, he stopped and watched Magnus Hanson at work, checking over his deep-sea fishing equipment.

The grizzled man squinted up at him. "What can I do for you, Mr. Calderon?"

"First of all, call me Simon."

"Simon it is. Come aboard, then."

As he did so, Simon noticed Magnus's scrawny mate, Elijah Greer, at the other end of the pier, huddled with a couple of hands from one of the cruisers.

"So, Magnus," he said without preamble, "tell me about my brother."

The captain nodded knowingly, as if he'd guessed Simon's reason for seeking him out. "Boone was a good man, he was. Good to his employees."

"What about women? Was he good to them?"

Magnus's rheumy blue eyes met his. "He was a man. Men have their failings. Thought he was changing his ways, though, with that Laughlin woman. Damn shame he didn't live long enough to find out."

No point in beating around the bush. "So you think he killed her...and himself?"

"I ain't no expert on such matters."

"You've lived long enough to judge how a person thinks. Is a good man capable of killing?"

A gruff sound akin to a laugh escaped the old sailor. "Any man can kill under the right circumstances."

As well he knew. "What about *these* circumstances?"

"Could be wrong, but I don't believe so."

"I don't think he did, either," Simon said, realizing he meant that without reservation. "But I think just about everyone else does. Including Elise."

He shook his head. "That poor girl had it bad for your brother."

"I noticed." Wondering who had the man's loyalty—his dead employer or a live young woman he obviously liked, Simon got to his purpose for the visit. "How long ago were they seeing each other? Before Blair?"

"That was the last time, far as I know."

"*Last?*" Simon echoed.

"They had an on-again, off-again kinda thing going. Whenever he was between women, Boone turned to Elise. Or let her in, I guess you could say."

Which sounded as if Elise's affections had never

been returned, something he hadn't expected. "Surely that couldn't have been enough for her."

Magnus guffawed. "Sex ever enough for any woman?"

Though Simon could think of one, he ruefully said, "Not usually."

"Ah, poor Elise. She took the crumbs. Actually, I think she kinda forced herself on your brother and he didn't fight her too hard. Maybe she figured if they were together enough, the relationship would take. Only it never did."

"Elise must have resented Audra, then."

"Didn't like her, that's for sure. Thought she wasn't good enough for Boone."

Simon doubted Elise would have thought any woman good enough for his brother...other than herself, of course.

Now the hard part.

"Did Elise ever say anything specific about Audra's taking Boone away from her?"

Magnus stared at him for a moment before saying, "Just 'cause I'm old don't mean I'm a fool. You want to know if I think she killed 'em, say so."

"Do you?"

Magnus flashed his decaying teeth at Simon in a weird grin. "Didn't say I'd answer." His gaze lifted to a spot above and behind Simon. "Make sure we got enough beer this trip out, would ya."

"Already did. And we do."

Simon glanced over his shoulder at Elijah, whose features were pulled into a disapproving frown.

How long had the mate been standing there, listening to their conversation?

And why exactly did he seem so unhappy?

PHOEBE LET THE PHONE ring until she wanted to scream. Where the heck was Simon? And why wasn't he trying to call her?

She felt like exploding. Here she had new, possibly important information and she didn't know what in the world to do with it. She'd even tried him at Calderon Charters but had missed him there, as well.

Noticing a party of four at her station, she slammed the receiver in its cradle and seated them.

If only she could have gotten something concrete out of Jimmy Bob Dortch. Like whether or not he'd planted the video equipment, either for himself—after his last admission about his loving Audra, she had to consider it—or for someone else; or whether he'd merely gone on a fishing expedition, looking for something of value to steal.

Then, again, the rest of the room hadn't seemed disturbed, as if the handyman had known exactly what he was looking for and where he'd find it.

Not that that was proof of anything.

For all Phoebe knew, Audra could have had that camera installed herself—a kinky if plausible explanation for its placement, and one the authorities would be likely to buy. She couldn't be sure they'd make the connection between someone else's interest in her sister's bedroom activities (as in her soon-to-be ex-husband) and her death.

And to tell the truth, Phoebe wasn't sure she could make the connection, either.

The thing that was really bothering her, though, went back to the journal entry—her sister thinking someone had been watching her in her own bedroom. The video camera would have provided the means for someone to watch without actually being present.

Bubba?

If he'd been picked up yet, Detective Sandstrom hadn't called to tell her. But thinking of him reminded her of the other phone call she'd been meaning to make—one to a certain Naples lawyer. She meant to confirm the connection between her brother-in-law and Bubba.

Returning to the telephone, she looked up the number and punched it in.

A moment later, a voice whose accent was distinctly New York answered, "Donald Platt's office."

"May I speak to Mr. Platt, please?"

"Sorry, honey, but Mr. P's not in at the moment. Wanna leave a message?"

Phoebe said, "Actually, I'm calling to confirm an appointment for Vance Laughlin. Do you think you can do that for me?"

"I think I can manage," the woman said dryly. "What day and time?"

"Tomorrow at three."

Only a few seconds passed before the secretary said, "Nope," as Phoebe had known she would. "No Laughlin on tomorrow's schedule."

"Oh, dear, he must have gotten the days confused," Phoebe said, trying to sound flustered. "Can you check the rest of the week and maybe next week…''

A big sigh was followed by a ''What was his name again?''

''Laughlin. Vance Laughlin.''

''Hang on.''

Disturbed that the woman didn't even know a client's name, Phoebe hoped this was strictly a case of incompetence. At least she was cooperating.

A moment later, the phone came alive again. ''Nope, not here, not anywhere in the next two weeks. Do you know when he made this appointment?''

Anxious now, Phoebe said, ''I believe the last time he was in the office. You could check Mr. Platt's personal calendar. He might have made a notation.''

''Oh, no, honey, that's impossible.''

''Why?''

''Because he's never been here before or I'd know him. I just figured Mr. P. made an appointment and entered it himself when I was on break or something.''

Uh-oh. ''He's tall, very fit, early forties.'' Phoebe was trying to speak calmly, so her tension didn't get through to the other woman. ''Dark brown hair with threads of silver at the temples—''

''Doesn't ring my chimes. Besides, we don't have a file on him, which means he's never been here, which means he's not our client. Look, honey, you got the wrong law office.''

Either that or Vance Laughlin wasn't the one who'd hired the lawyer to get his dirty work done.

But that couldn't be. Vance *had* to be the one behind the photographs.

"Are you certain?"

"As sure as my name is Dottie Rimes."

No sense in arguing with the woman. Thanking her, Phoebe hung up. More to tell Simon...if she ever connected with the man.

She tried his home number one more frustrating time. Ten fruitless rings later, she slammed the phone down.

After seating a couple, Phoebe wandered over to the bar and slid onto a stool.

Kevin gave her a once-over. "You're the picture of cheer this afternoon."

"If I wasn't working, I'd let you get me drunk."

"Thinking about Audra?"

"I'm always thinking about her. I rarely think about anything else."

She wasn't about to tell him that Simon was practically her only distraction from the double murder.

"It'll get easier."

"I don't want it to get easier. I want it to get solved." She hated the pity she recognized in his gaze. "Yeah, I know, you think I'm on a fool's errand."

"So-o-o, things aren't going the way you expected?"

Not having told Kevin about their close escape the night before—she neither wanted to hear an *I told you so* nor to worry him—she said, "Not exactly."

"I take it you didn't find this Bubba character, after all."

"Oh, we found him, all right. He was hired to follow Audra through a lawyer, but I can't make the connection to Vance. To make matters worse, I caught Jimmy Bob Dortch in Audra's bedroom and—"

"You what?"

"He was removing some video equipment."

"Jimmy Bob...stealing?"

"Or making X-rated home movies," she said, still not convinced. "I don't know what to think."

She gave him a quick rundown of what had transpired between the handyman and her that morning.

Kevin reached across the bar and took her hand. "Ah, Pheebs, I can't apologize enough—"

"Why should you?"

"I feel responsible. I recommended him to do the work. Tell you what. I'll see if I can't track him down first thing tomorrow. Maybe he'll talk to me."

"Thanks, Kevin."

"Hey, what are friends for?"

She should have taken him up on his offer to help in the first place, three heads being better than two...

For the next hour, Phoebe kept herself busy seating dinner guests. Among them was the dark-haired woman her partner had been coming on to the night before. She noticed him stopping at the woman's table. They talked for a few minutes before Kevin bent over and whispered something in her ear. The woman laughed and whispered back.

And so she was not surprised when Kevin approached her later, saying, "Hey, Pheebs, I have a chance for a hot date, but only if I can make it early."

Phoebe rolled her eyes at him. "I suppose I can handle things around here," she said with a mock-exasperated sigh. "Besides, you've been covering my butt for days. So, when she leaves—"

"Which seems to be right now."

"Go on with her."

"Pheebs, you're a peach."

"And you're a walking testament to testosterone," she muttered, slipping behind the bar.

At first, things ran smoothly, Phoebe splitting her time between acting as bartender and hostess, but her partner couldn't have been gone for more than an hour before she had cause to regret his absence.

About to return to the bar after seating a party of six, she turned around and ran smack into Vance Laughlin.

Immediately, she flew back, her heart pounding like mad. "What are you doing here?"

"Looking for you…and here you are." His visage darkened. "You have something of mine. No one takes what's mine and gets away with it."

Nearly panicking—thinking he'd known about the diary and had just found it missing—Phoebe tried to keep a cool head. "I told you I gave that locket to Audra when we were kids. It isn't worth anything to you."

"Screw the locket."

Pretending innocence, she asked, "Then what?"

"Don't play with me, Phoebe. You'll lose."

Her heart stalled out for a second. "I don't know what you're talking about, Vance. Furthermore, I don't have time for this."

She started to move away, but he caught her by the forearm with a cruel grip and spun her around.

"What the hell do you think you're doing?" she demanded, keeping her voice low, so as not to disturb the customers.

"I want that photograph," he told her. "And I want it now!"

Phoebe gaped at him, speechless until he tightened his grip. And though she struggled, she couldn't free herself.

"You're creating a scene," she said through clenched teeth.

He gave her arm a sharp twist that made her cry out and caught the attention of a couple at nearby table.

"I'll do more than create a scene—"

"Let go of the lady before I break your arm," came a low threat from behind them.

Phoebe glanced back to see Simon glowering at Vance, his narrowed gaze chilling. He appeared as dangerous as a man could.

And she'd never been so glad to see anyone in her life!

Chapter Twelve

Phoebe raised her eyes to the heavens and mouthed the words *thank you* even as Vance whirled around, asking, "Who the hell do you think you..."

His demand trailed off when he came face-to-face with Simon, and his grip loosened enough that Phoebe was able to pull herself free.

"The name's Calderon."

Stepping into Simon's shadow, Phoebe realized she'd never seen her brother-in-law look so spooked. She swore his tan paled and his eyes opened in horror.

"B-but...you're dead and buried."

"As you can see, I'm very much alive." Simon gave him what Phoebe thought of as an alligator grin. "Oh...you must be thinking of my brother Boone. I understand you were one of his biggest fans."

Vance cursed under his breath, then focused back on Phoebe. "The photograph!"

"Time for you to leave now, Laughlin," Simon told him in a voice as cold as steel. "Go pick on someone your own size. Maybe you want to start with me."

To Phoebe's delight, Simon exuded danger. An invisible power rippled from him, his intensity filling the space between them as effectively as if it were a tangible thing.

And while her brother-in-law seemed torn about whether or not to take him up on the offer, in the end, he backed down.

"We're not through," Vance promised Phoebe, but it was apparent to her that anything more than bluster had been knocked out of him.

"Get lost, Laughlin," Simon said in a voice low enough for only the three of them to hear, "before I decide to give you a hand straight into a swamp. I can make sure no one ever finds you."

With another curse, Vance left.

And a relieved Phoebe sagged into Simon, grateful for the steadying arm he put around her.

"Are you all right?"

"Yes, now that you're here."

Realizing she meant it in more than the physical sense, Phoebe grew restless. Rubbing her arm where Vance had brutalized her, she pulled away from Simon and moved toward the bar.

"What do you think Detective Sandstrom would say if I told him about this?"

"He'd probably threaten to arrest us for violating Laughlin's rights," Simon said, following close. "So he knows about the photograph."

"I can't believe he figured out it was missing. What does he do, fetch the envelope every night, pull out the photos and gloat over his victims?"

"My guess is Bubba's more greedy than we gave

him credit for. He's playing both sides of the fence, keeping his options open. I take it he hasn't been picked up."

"If he has, I haven't been informed."

Customer traffic had slowed now, as had the demand for drinks. They settled at the bar, Phoebe pulling a few beers, Simon drinking one. And as she worked, she filled him in on the situation with Jimmy Bob.

"The plot thickens," Simon said. "Maybe I should have a talk with your handyman, as well."

"Kevin already volunteered."

He looked around as if just realizing Kevin was gone. "Where is your partner?"

"Making time with that woman he was flirting with last night."

Simon raised his beer in salute. "Lucky man."

"You could have been lucky yourself," she reminded him, finally noticing how different he looked. How *good* he looked—clean-shaven and wearing casual dress clothes.

"Maybe I'm more particular," he said lightly. "And I want to be wanted for more than my body."

His body was nicely accentuated by pleated linen trousers and a collarless, long-sleeved white shirt.

Phoebe felt a flush creep through her, but she wasn't about to back down.

"Can't handle being the object of a woman's lust, huh?"

"I can handle it just fine." His eyelids drooped to their bedroom mode and he inched closer to her across the bar. "As long as my partner admits to more."

"What if there isn't more?" she asked stubbornly.

He smelled good, too. She'd never noticed him wearing a scent before, but tonight citrus mixed with musk pulsated from his every pore.

No wonder she felt a little light-headed.

"Then I pity her."

"Oh, please," she muttered, fighting the attraction for all she was worth. "I don't need this! Save your pity for misguided women like Audra or my mother."

"What do misguided women have to do with you and me?"

"Nothing directly," she said, wondering how the conversation had gone so far off track. "They just set bad examples. They give everything to a relationship and, in the end, they're left with nothing to show for it but a broken heart."

Phoebe couldn't believe this. They should be picking apart everything they'd learned in an effort to prove Vance had murdered their siblings—or had them murdered.

"You've got it all figured out, don't you?" he asked. "And so you're willing to chance nothing so you can protect yourself."

"Let's just say I'm smarter than other women in my family have been."

"If you were smarter, you would pick better men. Instead, you're cheating yourself."

And Simon seemed intent on ripping her apart.

"So you're telling me *you're* a better man?"

The way he was looking at her put a lump in

Phoebe's throat. What in the world did he want of her? She was who she was. Why couldn't he just leave it alone?

"How good a man I am is something for you to decide." He pushed away from the bar. "In the meantime, I'd better get a move on. I'm already fashionably late."

Remembering he'd made a date to have dinner with Boone's ex-fiancée, Phoebe bit back an unwelcome urge to snap at him. "Right. From what I remember, Blair Ratcliff doesn't like to be kept waiting."

"That's her problem."

And Simon was becoming hers, Phoebe realized, fighting an unexpected urge to panic when she recognized the searing flare ripping through her to be jealousy.

"What's the point?" she asked tersely.

"Of having dinner with a beautiful woman?"

"Well, when you put it like that—"

"I figure it'll be interesting."

"Right."

"But I'll be back to tell you all about it," he promised.

"Don't bother."

"I thought you wanted to find a murderer."

Phoebe gaped as the conversation came full circle. And decided to change her tune.

"What time?" she asked sweetly.

He smirked. "It all depends on Blair."

And then he left.

Leaving Phoebe glaring at his back, wanting to

throw something, and certain that Simon was purposely trying to drive her crazy.

THE WHARF HUNG OVER Naples Bay, nearly the entire restaurant having been built on its own pier. Simon entered via the street level bar nearly half-past nine.

He spotted Blair immediately. Surrounded by several others in her circle, she was holding court rather than blending into the crowd. And quite a queen she made, dressed in a chamois-colored dress that gave the illusion of nudity, and a stunning gold collar on which was set a large central topaz.

He knew she saw him but took pains not to recognize his presence. Obviously, she was waiting for him to interrupt, to make public his apologies for being late.

Instead, Simon parked himself near a potted ficus and waited for her to make the first move.

Which she quickly did.

With a smile fixed on her lovely face, she made her excuses and approached him.

"I thought you didn't like staying up late."

"Since you changed the time, I decided a nap was in order."

"Good. Then you'll be ready for…anything."

He could tell she felt challenged. Good. Keep her on her toes, unaware of his true purpose.

Blair had already arranged for a romantic table for two. On the way there, Simon felt a half-dozen pairs of eyes following them.

"You're giving people the willies," she murmured,

sounding pleased. "They think they're seeing a ghost."

"And you're loving every minute.

Her smiled confirmed it. Obviously she got off on rattling cages, starting with the parents who hadn't approved of her relationship with his brother. He recognized her type. She was used to having the upper hand.

Well, he was going to give it to her.

"So, Simon, what is it you do?"

"I live with nature as best I can."

"Well, here in southern Florida, we all do to some extent."

"But I do it in the swamps."

Her eyebrows arched. "I see."

"So, no potential here. Just shock value for the old folks."

"Excuse me?"

"No need, as far as I'm concerned," Simon assured her. "How long will it take Mommy and Daddy to find out you've done it again?"

Blair sighed. "They'll probably be waiting up to lecture me."

The arrival of a bottle of wine interrupted them.

Blair informed him that she'd already ordered for both of them and quickly added, "Hope you don't have any objections."

Figuring that would probably please her—and deciding to choose his battles—Simon shrugged and raised his glass in toast. "Whatever is good enough for the lady…"

After they'd both tasted and commented on the

quality of the wine, he steered the conversation back where they'd left off.

"I have a suggestion that beats boredom. Why not get a life, so you don't have to try so hard?"

A frowned marred the perfection of her face. "I have a life, thank you."

"I mean one that makes you happy. I'm a big believer in personal satisfaction."

The frown lightened. "You sound a lot like Boone."

"We were a lot alike." And he was becoming more comfortable with that.

Blair sipped at her wine then looked out to the bay, dark but for the lights of docked boats and surrounding restaurants. "I did care for your brother in my own way."

The first honest emotion Simon had felt from her.

"So you weren't quite so blasé about the breakup as you tried to make me believe."

"I am human."

"It must have been embarrassing at first, having to listen to your friends try to comfort you."

"I got through it by getting away from them. I took a cruise."

"The Keys?"

"I always go for the exotic. The Bahamas... Ja-
maica...Haiti..."

"Haiti," he echoed, the voodoo doll instantly springing to mind. "Interesting."

"Very," she agreed. "The scenery. The food. The culture."

"Religious aspects," he added as their appetizers were delivered.

Garlic shrimp, accent on the garlic. He bit back a smile and into his food.

Blair said, "I'm not exactly what you'd call a religious person."

"I would think you of all people would be intrigued by the black arts. Santeria. Voodoo."

"I was more interested in worshiping the sun during the day and being an object of worship at dance clubs at night."

Simon let the conversation lull for a moment while they worked on the shrimp.

He even refilled their wine glasses before casually saying, "You really didn't come into any contact with the black arts?"

Blair set down her glass and narrowed her gaze at him. "Hmm, I'm getting the distinct feeling this interest in mumbo-jumbo isn't casual."

"You wouldn't have brought back some unusual souvenir?" he went on. "A voodoo doll, for example?"

"Now why would I do that?"

"Because you hated Audra Laughlin?"

"I might make fun of lots of institutions, Simon, but death is not something I take lightly or that I would fool with."

"Someone did."

He told her about finding the doll.

"And you thought *I* was responsible?" She sounded indignant. "That's the reason for this dinner?"

"Truthfully, I didn't think any such thing until you mentioned the cruise and Haiti. Besides, who else would have reason to curse Audra?"

Blair sat back in her chair and snorted. "Try that twit, Elise Navarro. She plays the martyr, the faithful woman wronged, very well, when in fact Boone never had any serious interest in her."

"She thinks highly of you, too."

"She was always poking her nose into our business," Blair said. "You should be giving her and her uncle the third degree instead of me."

"Uncle?"

"The old man who works as a mate on one of the fishing boats. Elijah something or other."

"Elijah Greer is Elise's uncle?"

He'd realized Boone's assistant was of mixed heritage, of course, but he hadn't made that connection.

"Great-uncle, I believe. On her mother's side. The Cuban part comes from her father's family. Anyway, if anyone would know about voodoo dolls, old Elijah would be the one. He *is* from New Orleans."

No wonder the mate had looked at him so darkly after eavesdropping on his conversation with Magnus. Old Elijah was protective of his own blood.

Exactly how protective was the question...

PHOEBE DIDN'T WANT to have to think too hard on why Simon didn't come back for her as promised.

Could Blair hold the same fascination for him as she had for Boone?

Unable to think of another reason he'd want to be with the socialite in the first place, she admitted to unwelcome feelings of rivalry. Not that she stood a chance against someone as slick as Blair Ratcliff. All that talk of her being a woman scorned and therefore suspect was just talk. The socialite didn't care enough about anyone else to exert herself to get revenge.

And murder?

She might ruin her manicure...

Disgruntled on general principles, Phoebe locked up the moment the last table emptied. Within a quarter of an hour, she had what was left of her staff out the door and was headed for home herself.

No way was she going to wait around for Simon to show his face...if he ever did.

No way was she going to acknowledge her disappointment as being anything more than a desire to hang Audra and Boone's murders on Vance and make them stick.

Only...why did she feel as if her theory about her brother-in-law was unraveling?

Too many *ifs*.

Bubba...Donald Platt...Jimmy Bob Dortch...to name only three.

How did they fit into the picture?

Somehow, Phoebe was certain, they were all connected, but tonight she was too tired to figure it out. Hard enough to keep herself going, to keep her eyes open to drive, even with the top down.

Rather than waking her, the cool night air lulled her into longing for her own bed and a good night's sleep.

And if Simon Calderon had one lick of compassion for her, he'd stay the heck out of her dreams.

Yawns attacked her fast and furious as she turned into her development. Luckily, she could drive the winding route in her sleep.

Away from the denser segment of the complex and arriving within sight of her house, Phoebe reached for the passenger sunshade, attached to which was the controller for the automatic garage door opener. She pressed the Open button and slowed the convertible. Carefully, she slid into her parking spot, which had been narrowed considerably by several large boxes of unassembled shelving and office furniture she'd recently bought for her den.

She flicked the controller again to close the garage door, then cut the engine.

Not until the rolling door cut her off from the outside did she realize the interior garage light was out and that she was stranded in total darkness. Resourceful as usual, she opened the car door and used the courtesy light to identify the back door key.

About to slide out of the seat, she hesitated when something nearby stirred. The fine hairs on the backs of her arms raised, but hard as she strained to listen, Phoebe didn't hear the noise repeated.

No doubt some nocturnal animal was sniffing around the outside of the garage for food.

Anxious to get to her bed, she left the car and moved toward the door, her exhaustion making her clumsy. She knocked into a garbage can, sending a lid shooting off to land with a noisy clatter.

And then from the other side of the garage, another sound, this one far more sinister, froze her to the spot.

A hiss.

Not a faint hiss.

Too piercing.

No tiny, timid creature this.

Her mouth went dry and her fingers slipped so that she almost dropped the key ring. The noise of metal-on-metal seemed to echo through the garage.

Another hiss.

Too familiar.

How many times had she heard it in the swamp the night before?

A quick movement rattled the boxed furniture. Phoebe envisioned a large, scaly body lunging over the pile. She'd read about alligators getting locked in garages, one of those expected nuisances of living in a former swamp. The idea didn't thrill her.

Too scary to stick around to find out for sure.

Phoebe flew toward the door, fumbling fingers somehow managing to snap on her flashlight. Thankfully, she could see what she was doing when she shoved the key into the lock.

Problem was…the key wouldn't turn.

"Damn!"

What a time for the lock to stick. She tried again with no results.

"Double damn!"

Another scrabble and hiss in return—this one more threatening—made her jiggle the handle and throw her shoulder into the door, but neither budged.

More slithering…more hissing…getting closer… what to do?

Her worst nightmare lay not in the wilderness of Simon's swamp but in the civilization of her own garage. Shaking, Phoebe knew her only escape lay with her car, and that she had to get out fast before the thing got to her!

She flew back toward the open convertible, again knocking into the trash can, which toppled this time, spewing bags of garbage across the garage floor. Rotting food issued a siren's call to the creature, and it scrabbled closer...faster...seemingly scooting directly under the car.

Trying to keep her head, Phoebe jumped over the closed driver's door to get out of the way, whomping her left shin in the process. She landed in a tangled heap and fought tears of pain and fear.

Once securely seated, her heart pounding so loudly she couldn't hear the sounds from below, she had trouble making the key fit the ignition. Finally it took, and she started the engine. But in her haste reaching for the garage door opener, she knocked the control box straight off the sunshade and right out of the car.

"Triple damn!"

The motor was running, but if she wanted to get the car out of the garage, she needed the controller. Or she had to get to the switch next to the door. Either way, she'd have to chance meeting a hungry, maybe angry gator in the dark.

Then, again, she could just smash through her garage door...a very distinct possibility if she was left with no choice.

Wanting in the worst way to scream her frustration, Phoebe did just that. She opened her mouth and yelled, "He-el-lp! Someon-n-ne!" at the same time leaning on the car horn for all she was worth.

Chapter Thirteen

Blasts on a car horn and a woman's screams coming from Phoebe's place put wings to Simon's feet. He practically flew down the last hundred yards of the road to her garage and banged on the door.

"Phoebe!" he yelled. "What's going on?"

But she obviously couldn't hear over the din she was making.

Without a clue as to the trouble she was in, he was desperate.

The lanai!

Simon breached the screened door and expected he'd have to break the guest bathroom window to get inside the house. As he circled the pool, he swept his gaze around every corner, seeking out trouble but connecting with something odd instead.

Part of the sheer curtain at the breakfast nook bunched between the sliding glass door and the jam.

He raced to check it out.

Even as the door slid open, the horn blasts and screams for help stopped.

Heart pounding, praying Phoebe was alive and unhurt, Simon hit a bank of lights, then found the short hallway that led to the garage. The door stuck. Leaping up to grab onto a decorative ledge overhead and praying it would hold, he swung back and let his body carry his weight forward with his legs aimed straight at the door. Both feet rammed into the latch side hard enough to jolt his spine and snap his head back.

But with an explosion of sound, the panel ripped free of the frame and flew open. He landed in a crouch on the balls of his feet, ready to do battle, astonished at the sight that greeted him.

The convertible, top down and lights on, with Phoebe straddling the driver's seat and one aggressive and obviously aggravated alligator negotiating the bumper, seemingly determined to get at her.

"Simon!" came Phoebe's strangled-sounding call. "What do I do?"

Once the gator climbed onto the hood, she would be in real trouble, Simon knew. The creature moved fast and she had nowhere to go!

"Door opener?"

"At the wall!" she yelled, pointing.

Picking up the nearest loose object at hand—an old muddy shoe she'd left outside the door, Simon chucked it at the gator to give Phoebe an extra few seconds, while he danced around an overturned garbage can to get at the switch.

As he hit it, he said, "Back the car out."

"You want me to get into the driver's seat with an alligator on the hood?"

"He won't be for long."

Simon picked up the nearly empty garbage can and,

to dissuade the alligator from advancing, tossed it with a loud war cry. The can bounced off the beast, the remaining garbage splattering the windshield and fender.

Eyes glowing red in the semidarkness, the fierce reptile hissed at him, but slid off the hood.

''Now!'' Simon shouted.

Phoebe jumped back into the driver's seat and quickly put the car into gear. Backing it up before the door fully rose, she slid through the opening with mere inches to spare.

And, as he figured it would, the gator sniffed its freedom and made a swift dash for it, slinking out of the garage and disappearing into the dark.

Simon took a deep shuddering breath and let his tensed muscles relax. While alligators rarely went after humans, this one had been both riled and cornered. If he hadn't arrived in the nick of time—

Phoebe's head was bowed. Her forehead touched the steering wheel. She remained like that only for a moment before straightening and moving the car back into the garage. When she cut the engine, she sagged back into her seat.

''What the hell happened?'' he asked, hitting the switch to close the garage door.

''*I* happened,'' she said. ''I spoiled the gator's nap with all the noise I made coming home, I guess. He got a little annoyed with me.''

''The garage door was down?''

''No. I always leave an open invitation for swamp things to visit.''

''Then how did he get in here?''

"He could've been here for a couple of days for all I know. It happens. Only…"

"What?"

"I'd bet dollars to doughnuts the door lock never jammed on anyone else right after finding an unwelcome reptile in the garage."

"I couldn't open it from my side, either," a troubled Simon admitted. "That's why I had to kick in the door."

Which meant a closer inspection of the faulty mechanism might prove fruitless.

Why had a perfectly good lock jammed unless someone had helped it along?

Which would mean someone had wanted her to be locked in the garage with a pissed-off alligator…

The murderer.

That led to another string of questions, starting with how the perpetrator had gotten into Phoebe's house in the first place.

"You obviously need a security system," he said grimly. "I was able to get into the lanai without a problem, and—"

"Whoa!" Phoebe burst out of the car and slammed the door. "You're lecturing me?"

"*Someone* needs to be concerned about your safety."

Which he was, more than he cared to admit.

Phoebe stalked by him, but she stopped at the busted door and stared at it. Her shoulders sagged.

"My own personal commando to the rescue." Without looking at him, she muttered, "By the way, thanks."

"You're welcome, by the way."

Moving closer to her, Simon could see she was shaking and trying to hide the fact. Taking advantage of her momentary weakness, he pulled her around and pressed her into his chest where she unsuccessfully tried to hold back tears. Within seconds, his shirtfront was damp.

Simon stood there, patting Phoebe's back, thinking he should do more. *Wanting* to do more. He'd never felt so helpless. All he could do was let her cry.

Suddenly, she seemed to realize what she was doing. "Oh, no," she muttered with a sniff. "I'm ruining your good shirt."

"The shirt will survive."

Just as she had, thank God.

"I'm okay," she assured him between one last sob and a hiccup. "I tend to cry when I get mad and frustrated."

"You don't have to feel bad about letting out your emotions. An aggressive gator would have been enough to scare anyone."

"I wouldn't be so emotional if I wasn't so blind tired," she protested, ineffectually trying to free herself. "All I could think about all the way home was getting a good night's sleep."

"Shh," he murmured, refusing to let go, brushing his lips across the top of her head. "You don't have to explain."

Though he kind of liked her babbling. It was a soft side of Phoebe he hadn't seen nearly enough of. Not only did it turn him on physically, but it brought out his protective instincts, made him feel part of something.

Part of her.

He'd kept to himself too much, too long, and he was ready for a change. *For her.* Question was, did she return the feeling?

"I'm afraid if you let me go," Phoebe murmured, "I'll collapse into a puddle and not be able to get up."

"That's easy enough to fix."

Without warning, he lifted her into his arms and carried her inside the house. Despite the grim situation, a rueful smile twitched at his lips. He'd never thought of himself as hero material, but the moment—and this woman who'd gotten under his skin—gave him an inflated perspective.

He took Phoebe straight to her bedroom where he laid her gently on the bed. Her eyes were drooping as if she was ready to fall asleep instantly, but the feminine arms hooked around his neck were determinedly locked tight.

"Don't leave me," she whispered. "Not tonight."

A demand easy enough to obey. Simon had no desire to be anywhere but with her.

He couldn't get the broken door out of his mind. Couldn't forget the danger she'd been in. Couldn't forget the possible consequences.

He'd just lost a brother. A twin. Part of himself.

He couldn't chance losing her, too, not when he'd just found her. How had she become so important to him so quickly? Simon wondered.

He still didn't want to put words to the emotions

he was feeling. He was afraid she wouldn't return them, that he would scare her off before he had a chance to win her.

He flattened his hands on either side of Phoebe's shoulders, while asking, "What is it you want?"

"You."

"Why?"

"Because I need you right now."

He could have done without the *right now* part, but she'd said need, as well.

That's all Simon wanted to think about as he lowered himself onto her and took her mouth in a deep, soul-searching kiss. She responded in kind, nesting her body in the hollows of his, drawing the very breath from him, twisting his heart into unfamiliar knots.

He touched her as he'd wanted to every time he'd been near her the past few days. Face... throat...breasts...he took pleasure in claiming them all.

He wanted nothing more than to claim her completely right there.

Breaking the kiss, he murmured, "Phoebe, if anything had happened to you..."

"What? *You* weren't trying to chomp on me, though that's not a half-bad idea," she said suggestively.

But now was not the time for humor. Deadly serious, he told her, "I would never have forgiven myself for getting you into this."

"Uh-uh. *I* got *you* into this."

She pulled her smooth cheek across his clean-shaven one. She felt so damn soft. Helpless.

"But I should have known better," he went on. "I should have insisted we let the police handle the investigation."

He knew she wasn't helpless, of course. She was smart and resourceful.

But the killer was more so.

And the killer didn't have her sense of honor.

"You could have insisted all you wanted," she murmured. "I wouldn't have agreed."

"Then I would have made you."

Who could have tried to run them down? he wondered, the answer taking on increasing urgency. Who could have trapped an alligator in her garage?

"Two attempts on your life in two days." He shook his head in disbelief. "Letting this go on is unthinkable."

"Stopping now would be unthinkable."

"You're talking nonsense."

He thought about the voodoo doll. Elise. She could have handled the four-by-four, not the gator.

But Elijah could have.

Or Bubba...

Phoebe pushed at him and once freeing herself, rolled over. "Don't speak to me as if I'm a nitwit."

"Then don't act like one" was out of his mouth before he thought about it.

Still, he had a point. She wanted to steam ahead blindly, damn the consequences. He wasn't ready to sacrifice her...or let her sacrifice herself.

"I think you ought to leave."

"I'm not going anywhere."

"This *is* my house."

Temper rising, he demanded, "Is that how you solve all your relationship problems? If you can't win, you take your ball and go home?"

He wasn't the only one who was angry. Her hazel eyes blazed at him and her features hardened, sharpening the angles. And talk about body language—while only moments before, her shoulders had been slumped in defeat, her spine now seemed to be made of steel.

"Who's talking about a relationship here?" she demanded.

"*I* am. Or don't you ever want to have one with a man?"

"Not if it means that man gives me orders and expects me to follow them!"

"Even if it's in your best interest?"

"Not even then. I can decide what my own best interest is, thank you so much. I'm nothing like Audra."

Is that what she thought? That if she gave in to feelings and let someone have some say in her life that she would be like her sister?

"Then why do you keep comparing yourself to her?" he asked.

Her jaw tightened. "You can leave anytime."

"Get this straight—you're not Audra, and I'm not Boone."

He read the uncertainty deep in her eyes, bright with new, unshed tears. He thought she might soften.

But when she said, "Right, he didn't hide in a

swamp because he didn't want to deal with life," Simon knew he wasn't going to win, not tonight.

Possibly not ever.

"Then maybe I should disappear back into my swamp and stay there for good," he muttered, finally choosing to retreat. He slammed out of the house the way he'd come, yelling, "And lock this door behind me!"

Leaving via the lanai, he waited until he'd rounded the pool before glancing back. She was on the other side of the sliding door, doing as he'd ordered.

Thank God she had enough sense to realize *that* was in her best interest!

Simon was starting down the road toward his car before he cooled off enough to think rationally. If whoever had set up Phoebe with the gator wasn't still around, the person might be back to check on his handiwork. No matter how mad she made him, he couldn't leave her unprotected.

Detouring to the other side of the road, Simon headed straight for the giant old banyan tree, which had dropped dozens of roots that had taken in the soil and thickened. He could easily lose himself within the shelter of its maze and have a clear view of her place.

No matter that Phoebe thought she could take care of herself, he wouldn't abandon her until this matter was settled one way or the other. Someone had killed his twin and her half-sister. Someone obviously not averse to doubling his crime. Simon wouldn't rest until he saw justice done.

Making himself as comfortable as he could, he waited for the killer to return or for the sun to rise.

Whichever came first.

PHOEBE SPENT WHAT had to be the longest night in her life tossing and turning, getting out of bed and touring the house, checking the windows and doors—doing everything but sleep.

Well, maybe she slept a little. A few minutes here and there. Every time she drifted off, however, another ghost crashed her dreams.

A four-by-four vehicle on a rampage.

An alligator with a grudge.

Audra floating face down in a swimming pool.

Simon vowing to lose himself in a swamp.

Better to stay awake than to chance more nightmares.

If only she could make her mind stop playing tricks on her while awake. She kept seeing Simon in all his moods, kept feeling things best ignored, no matter how hard she tried to vanquish the memories.

Lack of sleep caught up to Phoebe at work the next day, when she seated the lunch crowd with as much enthusiasm as a zombie. Her lack of joie de vivre did not go unnoticed.

"See, this is what happens when I take an unscheduled night off," Kevin cheerfully chided her as she joined him during the late afternoon lull. "You work yourself so hard you become a basket case."

Her partner was sitting at a table between the ocean and the bar just in case he had to jump up to fill an order. Phoebe dumped herself in a chair opposite. She probably ought to tell him why she hadn't slept, but she didn't feel like going into it. Didn't want to hear another lecture like the one she'd had from Simon.

She gave a grin her best shot but figured it looked forced. "I look that good, huh?"

"You're letting the stress get to you, Pheebs." Kevin reached across the table and patted her hand. "But don't worry, no more advice from me."

"Not even of the romantic sort?"

"Did the word 'romantic' just pass your lips? Alert the media!" His expression knowing, he said, "So Simon Calderon got to you."

Phoebe ignored the obvious. She'd like to skip this discussion altogether. Then, again, Kevin was a good sounding board. She switched to a related topic that had been bugging her more and more lately.

"Do you think I'm like Audra?"

She hadn't thought so herself—not until she'd started reading her sister's diary and imagining herself with Boone's brother.

"I don't see much resemblance."

"Not looks. The kind of women we are." She frowned. "Or were, I guess."

Kevin's intense scrutiny made her shift in her seat. She wondered why the question bothered him so much, which it must considering he took his sweet time answering.

"That what Calderon thinks?" he finally asked.

She shook her head. "It's me. All me. I'm afraid of falling into the same traps that Audra did."

"I'm hearing it's already too late. Poor Pheebs. Just another besotted mortal."

Knowing that he was right—that Simon had too

quickly become more than an object of lust to her, she groaned. "Oh, Kev, what am I going to do?"

"Chill out, for one. You'll survive."

"How?"

"A clear head will help you sort it out. Getting some rest would be a good start."

"You mean now?" she asked incredulously. "I'm not bowing out on you again tonight."

"We won't get busy for a while. My place is your place, so to speak, so get your butt upstairs. Take a nap."

"Forget my trying to sleep."

"Then just veg out. Watch television. Relax. C'mon, you really do look like hell."

Not knowing what else to do, having all the energy of a turnip, Phoebe nodded. "It couldn't hurt."

"Good girl."

Once upstairs, she stretched out on Kevin's couch and tuned the television to the evening news. Oh, Lord, a couch had never felt so good.

She tried to concentrate on the anchorman's voice, but he seemed to drone on and on and on...

PHOEBE AWOKE to a room dark but for the square of blazing, moving light that, once she was able to focus properly, proved to be the television. She tried to concentrate on some comedy bit that, in the end, didn't seem in the least funny to her. Maybe she'd lost her sense of humor.

At first she didn't remember where she was. Then realization set in and she sat up with a jerk.

Kevin!

She'd left the burden of their business on him for yet another night. Several hours had passed. Why hadn't he sent someone to wake her up? At least she was feeling better—no doubt his purpose in leaving her alone. He was always looking out for her. A woman couldn't have a better friend.

Wanting to turn off the television, she looked for the controller, but it seemed to have disappeared. She snapped on a table lamp and searched all around. When the controller didn't surface, she figured the couch ate it while she was sleeping. Hopefully, Kevin could get the cushions to burp the darn thing up.

Phoebe stretched luxuriously and realized how much better she felt as she crossed to the entertainment center so she could turn off the set manually. She swore her partner had every electronic gadget around. In addition to equipment, he owned an amazing collection of CDs and videotapes. She automatically scanned them to see if he'd bought anything interesting.

A few X-rated video titles made her grin. And a few black boxes with names she recognized penciled in. Tourists he'd dated. Lovely ''magnetic'' girls to stand in when he couldn't get a live one to keep him company? As if that ever happened.

About to head back downstairs, one of those plain black boxes shoved behind the others, caught her eye.

Audra was scribbled across the label.

A weird feeling whispered through her.

Kevin had known her sister, of course. The three of them had shared dinner several times when Audra had started having trouble with Vance and would come to stay with her for a few days here and there. But why would he have a videotape of her?

Then it hit her. Jimmy Bob.

Kevin had promised to talk to the handyman, to straighten him out. She'd forgotten to ask him about it.

Thinking about Jimmy Bob Dortch taping her sister's private moments for his amusement made her queasy. Kevin must have confiscated this videotape from the man.

Feeling somewhat as she had when she'd first opened the diary, Phoebe turned the television back on and put the tape in the recorder for a quick look.

She had to know for sure...

Hand trembling, she pushed *Start,* then sat back on the floor. Her worst fears immediately confirmed, Phoebe averted her gaze from the screen.

About to stop the tape, she froze when she realized something important. Boone's hair had been dark, exactly like Simon's. This man's hair was fair.

Unable to help herself, she looked again, her focus going beyond the raw physical actions. The view gave a wide angle of the whole bed. The man's back was toward the camera. Even so, he was sickeningly familiar.

He rolled over, bringing Audra up over him, and in that instant, her worst fears were confirmed.

With a trembling hand, she stopped the tape.

How could she not have known?

Heart in her throat, she tore out of the apartment

and to her car, instinct driving her to find Simon, even as she heard Kevin call after her.

"Hey, Pheebs, wait up!"

She ran blindly and got behind the wheel.

She drove fast along the side streets of Marco. Her mind spun faster. Recounted an entry in the diary...

He's making life miserable for me. Won't accept that I've left him for good. That it's over. That I have no feelings for him...if I ever did.

She'd assumed Audra had been writing about Vance. That she was talking about her marriage being over.

Went for drinks with him. One last try to convince him in a civilized manner. He saw it as his chance to woo me back into his bed, into his life.

A bed she hadn't known Audra had slept in, Phoebe thought, finding it hard to breathe.

Why?

How could she have been so blind? How could Audra have been so secretive? Phoebe didn't need to hear her sister's voice to know. Audra had feared that Phoebe would disapprove—again. The same reason she hadn't said anything about Boone at first. Until she'd been sure of him.

More of the passage came to mind.

When I resisted, he turned ugly, acted like he could force me if he wanted to. I told him to go to hell and got home on my own.

A man capable of violence. But Vance, while psychologically abusive, had never been violent to her sister.

He doesn't care about me, really, just doesn't want to lose a trophy.

But I don't want to lose my sanity...or my life.

No, not Vance Laughlin.

Kevin Saltis.

It was her partner who treated women like trophies.

And unless she was horribly wrong, her partner and best friend was also a murderer.

SIMON AWOKE with a start. He hadn't meant to sleep this long, but he'd fought to stay awake all night and for a better part of the day to play guardian to Phoebe. Exhaustion had finally won the battle.

It had grown dark and the Blue Crab parking lot was nearly deserted. Tension drew him taut when he didn't immediately see Phoebe's convertible.

What he did see was her partner frantically tear down the stairs from his apartment and get into a sports car.

Saltis was going to leave with Phoebe already gone?

That didn't sit well.

Instinct drove Simon to follow even before Saltis drove out of the lot. Not wanting to be obvious, he'd left his truck on the side street and had hunkered down on the porch of a temporarily closed establishment. Fetching the vehicle, he was sorry he'd felt it necessary to stay out of Phoebe's line of fire.

Even so, he was able to play catch-up fast enough to spot the sports car zigzagging through traffic on the road back to the mainland. Only when he got there, Kevin Saltis didn't go north as Simon had expected.

He turned south.

Away from civilization.

Thoughts grim, Simon followed Phoebe's partner straight into the heart of his own territory.

Chapter Fourteen

That she was being followed didn't become obvious until Phoebe turned off the highway and onto the road that would take her to Simon's place.

The lights behind her swept low along the pavement.

A sports car.

Her heart thudded, but she told herself to calm down, that Kevin couldn't do anything to her once she found Simon. A little voice reminded her that he'd killed both her sister and Simon's brother, but she figured that happened only because they hadn't been forewarned, hadn't known what was coming.

But *she* knew.

Kevin was set on killing them both.

Phoebe practically cried for joy when she reached the narrow undeveloped side road that would take her straight in to Simon's place. And she almost wept real tears when she didn't see his truck. No vehicle sat parked on the crushed shell pad beneath his home.

What to do?

She couldn't go back. There was only that one way

in and out, and Kevin would be right behind her. A convertible with the top down offered no protection, as she'd discovered the night before.

She cut the engine and lights and left the car. Praying she would remember the path she'd taken with Simon, Phoebe decided to trust her fate to the swamp itself.

But before she got more than a few yards, the sports car swept in front of her and Kevin stuck his head out the window.

"Going somewhere?"

Phoebe froze to the spot as her partner alighted from the car, a gun in hand. He let the weapon hang at his side. For now.

Where the hell was Simon when she needed him?

"Why couldn't you leave well enough alone like I asked you to, Pheebs?"

Kevin positioned himself between her and the two vehicles. The moon gave her a clear view of his face. He appeared torn, as if he was already regretting what he was about to do. How gratifying.

"You should have listened to me," he went on. "I care about you, really. I'll never find another partner I like better. Then, again, it's time to sell the business and move on, maybe go solo next time."

"The police will track you down wherever you go."

Kevin laughed. "They've already let me get away with two murders."

All the anguish Phoebe had been feeling welled up in a single word: "Why?" She swallowed hard against the sickness that threatened her inside. "What did my sister ever do to you?"

"She used me. When she was still married to that creep Laughlin and she wanted some thrills, she came on to me."

"And you just couldn't resist."

"Hey, for once I tried out of respect for you. But Audra knew how to work a man to get what she wanted. She drove me crazy with lust until I would do anything she asked. Every time was better than the last. Her arsenal of tricks was spectacular, I must admit. I couldn't think about anything else. And then one day she walked away from me straight into Boone Calderon's arms. Giving her time to get tired of him was my big mistake."

As if he could force a woman to love him in return.

"You're the one who had her followed and photographed." Not to mention videotaped. When he merely shrugged in agreement, Phoebe added, "And you started to see that Audra wasn't going to tire of Boone."

"And I couldn't stop wanting her. You don't know what it's like when every waking moment, every dream is filled with one person. Someone you can't have."

"Oh, I have some idea," she countered, thinking of the way Simon had withheld what she'd thought she wanted from him.

"Your sister obsessed me, tormented me. And then paraded that swamp boy around like I had no feelings."

"Audra wasn't a cruel person. And she was in love."

"She was a selfish bitch!" Kevin insisted. "You asked me if you're like her. No, Pheebs, you're everything she wasn't. It should have been you I fell for, not her. Then none of this would have happened."

Or *she* would have been the dead one, Phoebe thought, since she would never have loved him in return. At least, not the kind of love that led a woman to a man's bed and made her want to stay there forever. Simon was the only man she'd ever met who'd made her think she was ready to take that chance.

She *did* love Simon, Phoebe realized. And if she was brave enough—and lucky enough to remain alive—she would tell him so.

Maybe *then* he would bed her.

But first she had to figure out how to stay alive long enough to find out.

"I'm not your type, Kevin."

She was stalling, looking around for an escape route.

"No, Pheebs, you're not. You're more like the kid sister I never had."

The words made her shiver. And yet...

"I felt like you were the brother I'd always wanted." The truth. As a man who hadn't threatened her, he'd been able to get closer to her than anyone but Audra. "Why, Kev? Why couldn't you have left Audra alone, let her be really happy for once in her life?"

"I would have done anything for her. She was a

fever in my blood. I told her that, tried to make her see I was the right man for her.''

''She would never have left Boone.''

''But I had to have her.''

''So you *killed* her because you couldn't have her?''

''I only meant to kill him. I figured if something happened to Calderon, she'd turn to me for comfort.''

Audra wouldn't have gone back to Kevin. The diary had made that clear.

''So you planned it.'' Suddenly seeing an escape on the other side of the house—a trio of airboats lined up along the dock, she started fidgeting, pacing, subtly moving closer to her goal. ''What went wrong?''

''I came up behind Calderon while he was sleeping in a lounge chair. I held a gun to his head in a way that would look like suicide…and then I pulled the trigger.''

Kevin's absorption in his tale gave her the freedom to move more directly in line with the airboats.

One quick dash…

''I didn't know anyone was there until I heard her scream. I didn't even mean to kill her. I just reacted. Raised the gun and shot. She was at the edge on the other side of the pool and fell right in. Then I dumped Calderon's body and dropped the gun in the water. Cleanup was easy with so much water around.''

''You got lucky,'' she said sarcastically, starting to focus for her run to freedom. ''How do you sleep at night?''

''As best I can. It's getting easier.''

''Will killing me be easier, too?''

"I'll survive it," he muttered.

Sensing some doubt in him, she jumped on it. "But face-to-face, Kev? Too bad old Bubba didn't finish the job for you."

"Bubba doesn't know that I exist. I gave you a fifteen-minute head start to the Osprey Nest, where I 'borrowed' what should have been a death-mobile."

"Did you borrow the alligator, too?"

"I hired a couple of guys who wrestle alligators as a hobby to play a joke on a friend. I took care of the lock myself."

Muscles taut, ready to sprint for freedom, she was waiting for her opening. "Just imagine your surprise when I showed up this morning."

"Part of me was relieved. I thought it was a sign, hoped maybe you'd leave it alone now. But then you found the videotape."

"I thought you got it from Jimmy Bob until I took a look for myself."

"He was getting the equipment back for me as a favor. I told him if anyone found it, people would think Miss Audra wasn't a nice woman. Besotted bastard didn't want that. I might not have known you'd found the videotape at all if you hadn't left it in the machine…now you've left me with no choice. Sorry, Pheebs, but your luck just ran out. Now it's your turn to die. For real."

Kevin glanced away from her as he removed the safety on his gun—just the break Phoebe had been waiting for. She flew under the house along the carport, crushed shells crunching beneath her sneakers.

She barely heard Kevin's "You won't get away

this time, Pheebs'' over the pressure of her own racing pulse filling her ears.

She did, however, hear the sharp discharge of his gun and feel the breath of the bullet as it whizzed by the side of her face.

THE GUNSHOT HURTLED Simon forward to the opening in the Glades, but he wasn't prepared for the sight of Phoebe jumping into an airboat, an armed Saltis on her heels.

Damn the near-blind old man who'd had no business driving at night and had caused a minor traffic altercation that had been impossible to get around. Realizing where Saltis was headed, Simon had abandoned the truck and had continued his pursuit on foot, taking a shortcut through the swamp.

The airboat roared to life and pulled away from the dock, more shots following, even as Simon flew forward, keeping to the shadows as he stalked Phoebe's partner.

Saltis commandeered the next boat in line—the one with the faulty starter. He didn't waste much time at it, but even those precious seconds gave Phoebe a respectable lead. Her partner shot off a few more rounds, before abandoning the cranky airboat for the third.

Surely he didn't have many bullets left. Not that it made him any less dangerous. Kevin Saltis had a powerful build—he could kill Phoebe with his bare hands.

Simon couldn't get to the dock fast enough to keep him from getting away. The bastard was off like a bullet, leaving him to kick-start the airboat with the faulty engine, and pray that he'd be able to run interference for the woman he loved before it was too late.

PHOEBE SPED ACROSS open water toward the maze of narrow channels that cut through the mangroves, knowing she was already lost. Once in, she'd never find her way out, but maybe that was a good thing.

Maybe Kevin wouldn't be able to find his way, either.

Jerking the rudder, she made a too-sharp turn, considering her lack of expertise. The craft slid around sideways and sent up a sheet of water over what looked to be a couple of logs, but she knew the "logs" to be alligators. The airboat threatened to swamp her, turn her into gator bait.

Refusing to succumb without a fight, she lifted her foot from the accelerator and finessed the rudder. The hull righted itself with surprising ease. She took the next curves slower, accelerating down long stretches.

She should have lost Kevin. Instead, she heard his engine more distinctly even through the padded ear covers. He had to be getting closer. Sometimes it even sounded like *two* engines.

A narrower channel set between the mangroves lay just ahead. She took it, then charged down another that was practically claustrophobic. She glanced back briefly—and turned forward just as the airboat plowed into a spiderweb that spanned the channel bank to bank.

Foot popping off the accelerator, Phoebe shrieked

and fought not only the silken threads, but several large black-and-white striped spiders, as well. One crawled down her back where she couldn't reach it. Another dropped from her shoulder to the boat floor—Phoebe prayed it wouldn't crawl up her pant leg. A third got tangled in her hair. She could feel it swinging against her neck.

"Ah-h-h!"

She leaned over the boat and shook her head until the damn thing dropped off into the water. Then she flapped her shirt until the one on her back freed itself. Her flesh crawled as she stared ahead where several more mega-webs, complete with occupants criss-crossed the channel.

Behind her...the sound of an engine drawing closer.

No choice!

Using a curved arm to shelter her face, she ducked low in her seat and stomped on the accelerator, trying not to retch as she felt enveloped and crawled upon.

Once through the labyrinth, she let up on the gas long enough to shake loose everything that didn't belong to her before taking off again.

But Kevin had zeroed in on her and the distance between them was closing. A bullet whizzed by. And another pinged against the metal hull. Phoebe made a run for it but couldn't lose him in the network of passages again.

Then she zigged when she should have zagged and found herself in open water—a prime target!

A glance back revealed not only Kevin on her tail,

but the silhouette of another airboat farther back. She didn't need to see the man to know who followed.

"Simon!"

By some miracle, he'd answered her silent call.

Thinking all she had to do was keep Kevin at bay long enough for Simon to catch up to them, Phoebe was horrified when she approached a section of saw-grass prairie that, oddly, rose higher than she sat. The stuff normally grew only to three or four feet. Circling to stay in clear water would take her back in Kevin's path.

Again left with no real choice, she jammed down on the accelerator. The airboat's shallow metal hull lifted fractionally as it darted forward, cutting a path through the fragile environment. She'd heard of patches that grew to a dozen feet—this was some-where in between.

Whipping across the river of grass, she felt as if she'd entered a different world.

Isolated. Dreamlike.

But it wasn't long before she was brought back to reality with a jolt.

Her engine coughed once, and then her craft bucked and stalled out.

Phoebe hit the starter. No response. She tried not to panic as her vehicle floated to a decisive stop.

Her situation was desperate.

She'd just run out of gas.

SIMON COULDN'T PINPOINT the exact moment the other airboats stopped, but he gradually realized he no longer heard their engines. Had Saltis caught up to Phoebe? He'd disappeared from view.

Without warning, Simon was upon the other two craft, both abandoned. He swerved to miss them and came to a dead stop a dozen yards distant. Tearing off his headset and jumping down to the wetland, he took stock of the situation. His eyes were better than most at night, and fortunately the moon was cooperating.

He expected Phoebe had taken off on foot with Saltis right behind. He could see the impressions made by their bodies as they tunneled through the saw grass. His hearing was as finely tuned as that of any swamper, and they weren't trying to be quiet.

Simon followed through wedge-shaped blades so high and thickly rooted together that a man could lose himself. Their sharp edges could also be nasty, and he steeled himself against the occasional sting.

As if in a dream, the landscape suddenly shifted, the grasses shorter, sparser. His heart pumped like mad when he recognized the hardwood hammock rising above the wetlands. Though the Glades constantly shifted and changed, he would never forget where the swamp had claimed his father.

A screech set his skin crawling.

"Let go of me!" Phoebe shouted.

And suddenly he was upon them.

Kevin was dragging a kicking, screaming Phoebe toward the willows limning the hammock. Knowing what lay ahead, Simon gathered all his forces.

With a feral grin, he attacked.

SIMON'S WAR CRY was followed by a jolt that freed Phoebe from Kevin's grasp and sent her reeling toward what looked like open water. She tried to stop herself, but she was breathless and staggering, not in control of her own body.

Landing with a splash, she looked up to see the two men locked in a deadly dance, Simon holding Kevin's gun hand out to the side. The weapon misfired. Kevin's arm jerked. The gun went flying and plunked into the water somewhere to Phoebe's right.

Having gotten her breath back, she tried to rise, but the bottom was mushy. The mud sucked at her sneakers and got hold of her feet. Trying to move forward, she felt as if she were sinking instead.

"Oh, no!"

Couldn't be.

She told herself not to panic—but when she tried to move one foot, the other sank to the ankle. And in trying to pull that foot free, the other leg became trapped nearly to her calf. It was no use. With her every movement, the swamp seemed more determined to suck her farther down, an inch at a time.

Horrified, Phoebe stared at the struggle on the grasslands through eyes that filled with tears. Kevin seemed to be choking the life out of Simon.

They were both going to die and no one would ever know…

Then Simon suddenly exploded with strength, his forearms knocking into Kevin's, effectively breaking the death grip of the other man's fingers.

Simon smashed the heel of his hand into Kevin's

face. Her partner screamed and something dark and wet spurted over Simon.

Blood from a broken nose?

Hands to his face, he fell back, at least temporarily incapacitated.

"Phoebe?" Simon called, his voice hoarse. "Are you all right?"

"Over here. I'm—ah-h—stuck."

"Don't move!"

Hearing the panic in his tone did not reassure her. "Trust me, I'm trying not to."

"I'll find something for you to grab."

He was already searching the ground frantically.

And despite the fact that she stayed put, hardly breathed, Phoebe continued to sink.

To the top of her knees...

The middle of her thighs...

The bottom of her buttocks...

She closed her eyes and prayed as the muck squiggled up around her hips.

"Got it!"

"Thank you," she breathed as Simon held out what appeared to be a gnarled root several feet in length. She curled her fingers around it. "Got it," she echoed gratefully.

"Hang on and let me do the work. If you struggle..."

He didn't have to finish. Struggling would sink her farther.

Simon started to inch back. Slowly. Steadily.

The root started to slip through her hands.

Phoebe tightened her grip, then felt the muck budge

as her upper body stretched out over the water toward Simon.

''It's working!'' she gasped as she felt her lower body lift slightly.

Simon kept on.

He inched backward. She slid forward.

He pulled. She hung on, her hands burning with the strain.

Then Simon stopped moving, dug in his heels and started pulling at the root, one hand over the other.

Her buttocks popped free...

Then her thighs...

Then her knees...

She was practically lying across the water, half of her freed when her hands came within reach of his.

He stepped forward and grabbed onto her wrists. She grabbed onto his in return, sealing their fates together.

When he started to pull again, her arms felt as if they would separate from her shoulders, but she clenched her jaw against the pain and felt her calves slip free.

''I'll anchor and you pull,'' Simon ordered.

For once she did as she was told without question.

Suddenly the swamp gave up its hold and freed her completely.

Tautness gone, Simon went crashing onto his back in the grass with her atop him.

''You did it!'' she cried.

Not their night to die, after all.

''This time,'' he said roughly, wrapping his arms around her back. ''Thank God.''

He had to be thinking of that other time when he'd been unable to save his father. Maybe some of that burden of guilt would lift from his shoulders now. She hoped so.

Suddenly, she said, "Kevin!" and glanced around frantically. "He's gone!"

"I doubt he'll get far."

Prophetic words.

Even as Simon got to his feet and helped her up, a roar of sound raised the hair on her head.

"What—"

"Gators. Probably bulls."

And then frantic inhuman screams and snapping sounds made her blood run cold. She clutched Simon until the screams stopped.

The snapping continued.

The swamp had provided them with a wild brand of justice that she never could have imagined.

PHOEBE WASN'T CERTAIN she would ever get over Audra's murder and so determined that group counseling with other people who'd lost family members to violence was in order. At least now she could focus on something other than finding the real killer.

The videotape and the diary she'd found in the shoe box—an account of Audra's affair with Kevin, which had ended when she'd begun to fear him—together with her and Simon's firsthand account were more than enough for the authorities and the media to change their tune.

Simon hadn't said a word about the diary when she

produced it. But the look of disappointment he gave her was enough to break her heart.

Then he disappeared back into his swamp.

Phoebe waited two days—long enough for him sleep off the exhaustion and stress—and when he didn't show his face, she decided whatever was going to happen in this relationship was up to her.

Relationship…

What should have been a scary concept now intrigued her. She'd gone through so much over the past week that she couldn't imagine her world ever being the same. Couldn't imagine being alone again, content with short-lived, comfortable affairs.

She wanted to share and fight and most of all love, and she only wanted to do that with one man, Simon, who had risked everything for her.

And so she was waiting for him on the screened porch and getting to know Minerva and Serena when he brought in an airboat after a morning of taking tourists fishing.

He couldn't miss her convertible parked on the pad. That he knew she was there was obvious from the set of his shoulders, though he avoided looking for her.

She gave each of the parrots treats and scratched their necks as she'd seen Simon do.

"So what do you think, girls?" she asked them. "Could you stand some extra attention on a regular basis?"

"Awwwk, Simon says no. Simon says no."

"We'll see about that," she muttered, when in her heart it was her greatest fear.

"See about what?"

He'd sneaked up on her. She turned around to face him. Leaning against the doorjamb, he was dressed in an old T-shirt and ripped jeans, his face sported at least a ten-o'clock shadow, and his eyes...oh, they were issuing an invitation that no part of her could resist. Tension suddenly radiated from her every pore.

"We'll see whether you're ready to take me to bed and keep me there until I'm unable to walk away."

He didn't move but asked again, "Why, Phoebe?"

She took a deep breath. This was the moment. The scariest one in her life. But she knew how she felt about him now and had sworn she would tell him.

"Because I love you, Simon Calderon, and I want it all. The sharing. The fighting. The sex." Pointedly, she said, "*Especially* the sex."

"Simon says no! Awwwk!"

"Shut up, you silly bird," Simon muttered as he finally made his move. He slipped his hands around Phoebe's waist and pulled her to him tightly. "Simon says yes. A very definite yes."

Epilogue

"So did they or didn't they?" Alex asked, when Zoe had finished relating Phoebe and Simon's story.

Knowing full well what he meant, Zoe focused on her folder when she murmured, "What?"

She busied herself with the Lust file, straightening articles and reports and copies of diary pages that were already in perfect order.

"Did they satisfy their lust for each other?"

"I certainly hope so." She carefully set the folder in her briefcase. "My records indicate that they married."

"Then I certainly hope they're still trying."

Hearing the amusement in Alex's tone, Zoe gave him a swift look, but his expression was perfectly innocent.

"Shall we partake?" he asked.

"Excuse me?"

"The dessert. It appears quite...tempting."

But Alex wasn't looking at the dessert. He was staring at *her*. Or perhaps she should say he was staring at her as if *she* were the dessert.

Zoe put it to his reaction to the case, which had, in fact, intrigued her more than she would admit. She'd been hard-pressed not to fantasize exactly as Phoebe had done. That Alex's image had come to mind with each passage meant only that she needed to get a social life.

At the moment, Alex Gotham was the only single man she was seeing in any capacity.

Zoe dug into her dessert, a sensual raspberry brûlée, and kept their conversation on track. "So, do you have enough information for the chapter on lust?"

"I may have to do some personal research."

Was he really toying with her or was she reading meanings where he meant none?

Shifting to find a comfort zone, Zoe chose to believe the second option.

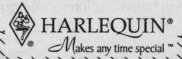

Sexy, desirable and...a daddy?

THE AUSTRALIANS

Stories of romance Australian-style, guaranteed to fulfill that sense of adventure!

This February 1999 look for

Baby Down Under

by **Ann Charlton**

Riley Templeton was a hotshot Queensland lawyer with a reputation for ruthlessness and a weakness for curvaceous blondes. Alexandra Page was everything that Riley *wasn't* looking for in a woman, but when she finds a baby on her doorstep that leads her to the dashing lawyer, he begins to see the virtues of brunettes—and babies!

The Wonder from Down Under: where spirited women win the hearts of Australia's most independent men!

Available February 1999
at your favorite retail outlet.

HARLEQUIN®
Makes any time special ™

My Secret Admirer

Savor the magic of love
with three new romances
from top-selling authors
**Anne Stuart,
Vicki Lewis Thompson and
Marisa Carroll.**

My Secret Admirer is a unique collection
of three brand-new stories featuring passionate
secret admirers. Celebrate Valentine's Day with
these wonderfully romantic tales that are
ideally suited for this special time!

Available in February 1999 at your favorite retail outlet.

HARLEQUIN®
Makes any time special ™

HARLEQUIN®

I N T R I G U E®

COMING NEXT MONTH

#501 A COWBOY'S HONOR by Laura Gordon
The Cowboy Code
Cameron McQuaid was both a cowboy and a lawman, and lived his life by a code of honor. Yet, when Frani Landon comes to town to catch a killer, Cameron finds his honor—and his heart—on the line.

#502 FAMILIAR VALENTINE by Caroline Burnes
Fear Familiar
A velvet Valentine's night, a threatening attacker—and suddenly, Celeste Levert found herself swept to safety in Dan Morgan's strong arms. He promised to keep her safe and secure, but couldn't offer his heart—until a black cat played Cupid....

#503 LAWMAN LOVER by Saranne Dawson
Michael Quinn's tenacity made him an extraordinary cop. It also made him an exceptional lover. And Amanda Sturdevant remembered everything, every caress and kiss, of her one night with him, but nothing of a long-ago night of terror that had left a woman dead and Amanda barely with her life—and amnesia....

#504 JACKSON'S WOMAN by Judi Lind
Her Protector
Everyone called her Verity McBride, but only Vera knew no one would believe the truth about her identity. But now with a murder charge hanging over her head, she turned to Jericho Jackson for help and found a love for all time—even though he thought she was someone else....

Look us up on-line at: http://www.romance.net